MANDIE
AND THE
SILENT
CATACOMBS

Mandie Mysteries

MANDIE
AND THE
SILENT
CATACOMBS

Lois Gladys Leppard

BETHANY HOUSE PUBLISHERS
MINNEAPOLIS, MINNESOTA 55438

Mandie and the Silent Catacombs
Lois Gladys Leppard

Library of Congress Catalog Card Number 90-055638

ISBN 1-55661-148-X

Published by Bethany House Publishers
A Ministry of Bethany Fellowship, Inc.
6820 Auto Club Road, Minneapolis, Minnesota 55438

Printed in the United States of America

This book has got to be for

Andy Unseth,

Who "bears all" without a complaint.

About the Author

LOIS GLADYS LEPPARD has been a Federal Civil Service employee in various countries around the world. She makes her home in Greenville, South Carolina.

The stories of her own mother's childhood are the basis for many of the incidents incorporated in this series.

Contents

Thou shalt not steal.
Exodus 20:15

Chapter 1 / Express Train to Rome

Mandie Shaw was quickly scanning the people in the train station in Paris, France, when her grandmother called to her.

"Amanda! Come on!" Mrs. Taft spoke sharply. "Senator Morton has our tickets, and we don't want to get separated in this crowd. Hurry up."

"I'm sorry, Grandmother," Mandie quickly replied. She hastened to join her friends, Celia Hamilton and Jonathan Guyer, who were trying to keep up with Mrs. Taft and Senator Morton.

"Celia, Jonathan," Mandie said in a loud, breathless whisper. "Did y'all feel someone watching us just now?"

Jonathan glanced at Mandie and laughed. "*Feel* someone watching us? Just how does one accomplish that?"

"It's an instinct, I suppose," Mandie replied, holding on to her white kitten, Snowball, as she walked along with her friends. "Maybe it's because I'm part Cherokee that I have that—what would you call it—the ability to feel someone watching. Anyway, this isn't the first time I've had that feeling over the years."

"All thirteen of your years?" Jonathan teased.

"Well, you aren't much older than I am, Jonathan Guyer," Mandie reminded him. "In fact you were only fourteen in January this year."

"Mandie, I believe you ... that someone is watching us," Celia said. "I felt it, too."

"You did?" Mandie replied. She turned back to Jonathan. "Then I was right. There was someone watching us. And you'd better believe us, Jonathan, and help us look out for whoever it was."

"All right, all right," Jonathan told her as they approached the platform where the hissing train was waiting.

They followed the adults up the two steps and into the passenger car. "This sure is a long train, and it looks so big, compared with ours back in North Carolina," Mandie commented as they continued on into a compartment.

"It's a lot different, I'm sure," Jonathan said.

Mrs. Taft and the senator sat down and motioned for the young people to sit on the long seat across from them.

"The inside is different, too," Celia agreed. "We don't have compartments like this in our trains at home in Virginia." Celia was Mandie's roommate at the private school they attended in Asheville, North Carolina.

"Grandmother, will this train take us all the way to Rome, Italy?" Mandie asked, rubbing Snowball's head as he squirmed in her lap.

"No, dear," Mrs. Taft replied. "This train will only go to the border and there we'll board the Italian express train for the rest of the trip."

"Just think. We're going into another country on a train," Mandie said. "We left the United States on a ship, and when we got to London, we took a ferry boat across the English Channel to France, and now we're traveling on a train." Mandie and Celia were on a tour of Europe in the summer of 1901 with Mandie's grandmother and Senator Morton, a family friend.

"Don't forget your journals, girls," Senator Morton reminded them. "You should write things down as they happen, before the freshness wears off."

"Yes, sir," Mandie agreed. "I hate to tell you this, but my journal is packed in my luggage, and I can't get to it right now. But I will keep it out from now on as we travel."

"Mine is, too," Celia added. "Mandie, if we each had a bag to put them in, they would be easier to handle, especially for you since you have your cat."

Jonathan spoke up. "I know just what you girls need," he said. "As soon as we get to Rome, I'll show you. There are shops in Italy that sell mesh bags that fold up and fit in your purse, or they will stretch out to carry things this big." He held his hands about a foot apart.

"Jonathan, I'm so glad we found you on the ship," Mandie told him. "You are such an experienced traveler. You seem to know everything. Have you gone to school in Italy, too?"

"Oh, no, not Italy," Jonathan replied, flashing his mischievous smile. "But I have traveled some in Italy. And before you ask me, I do not speak Italian, only French and English."

Mandie and Celia had found Jonathan on the ship they had taken from the United States to England. Although Jonathan had an aunt and uncle in Paris, where he was supposed to stay until his father came for him, Senator Morton had been unable to contact the relatives, who were out of town.

Senator Morton did get in touch with Jonathan's father, a wealthy businessman in New York, who had asked the senator to keep Jonathan with him as they traveled.

"I guess we're out of luck, then, unless my grandmother or the senator can speak Italian," Mandie said, looking across the aisle at the adults.

Mrs. Taft shook her head. "No, dear, I don't speak Italian except for a few words. But most of the people there speak enough French, and some English, that we won't have any trouble getting around." She looked at the senator. "Perhaps you speak Italian, Senator Morton?"

"A little," he admitted. "I'm not too good at it, but I can make myself understood sometimes. Actually, I can understand the Italians better than they can me."

"Senator Morton, what about all those other countries we're going to?" Mandie asked. "Switzerland, Germany, the Netherlands, Belgium, Scotland, Wales, Ireland—will you be able to translate for us when they don't understand or speak English?"

"Don't worry your pretty head about it, Miss Amanda. We'll manage," the senator assured her. "I've traveled quite a bit in Europe, and so has your grandmother. If the people don't understand what we say, we can always use our hands. The Italians, especially, use a lot of hand motions when they speak."

Suddenly the train whistle blasted, and the car jerked forward.

"Goodness!" Celia clutched the seat as the train began to speed down the track.

Mandie laughed. "You said this ride would be different, and it is," she said over the roar of the rattling, whistling train. "As fast as this thing is going, we should be there soon."

Jonathan smiled and nodded. "Soon, I suppose, but it's an awfully long trip—hours and hours."

The girls had never been on an express train before. The only ones they had ridden were the slow-moving ones up and down the eastern seaboard in the United States. They went slow enough for a person to take in the scenery along the way. This train went so fast it was impossible to enjoy the view. The telegraph poles along the way seemed to fly by too rapidly to even be counted.

The train was noisy, too, with all the rattle and roar of the speeding wheels. It was impossible to carry on a conversation without shouting at each other.

Many hours later, when the train finally came to a screeching halt at the border to Italy, the young people, dozing in their seats, were caught unawares. As it bumped to a stop in the depot they were thrown together. They all laughed.

"Whew!" Mandie breathed with a loud gasp. "I'm sure glad that's over and done with." She clutched Snowball, who was also frightened by the sudden stop.

Mrs. Taft and the senator were sitting in separate seats with arms on each side of them and they looked at the young people and laughed.

"I should have warned you," Mrs. Taft said. "When you sit on that long bench-type seat there's nothing to hold on to."

"We'll warn you next time," the senator told them as they all got up.

Mandie eagerly looked out the window. All she could see was the depot platform, as she and her friends followed the adults down the aisle to the train steps, carrying their bags.

"We must hurry," the senator urged them down the steps. "I believe that's our train there on the next track." He indicated a long black train which sat huffing and puffing and faced in the direction they were going.

As they boarded the train to go into Italy, the conductor stood at the entrance checking papers and tickets. The adults showed him whatever he needed to see as the young people waited and watched. The man kept chattering away in what Jonathan said was Italian.

Handing the papers back to Senator Morton the man smiled and said, "*Da questa parte*," as he indicated with his hand that they should board the train.

Mandie climbed the few steps behind the adults, then turned and smiled at the man and said, "Thank you."

The man burst into a big smile, bowed slightly and said, "*Grazie*." Then he added in English, "Thank you. Welcome to *Italia*."

Mandie was so thrilled with having conversed with a real Italian that Celia had to push her to go ahead.

"He understood English," Mandie said excitedly as she followed the others through the train car and into a compartment. This one was larger and much fancier than the one on the French railway. And Mandie noticed the seats had arm rests. They wouldn't be thrown around on this train because they'd have something to hold on to.

"I do hope we can see some of the countryside this time," Celia remarked, as they sat down.

"You'd better plan on seeing the countryside from

somewhere besides a train," Jonathan told her, laughing.

"Do you mean we're going for another fast train ride?" Mandie asked, uneasily holding on to Snowball.

"I'd say faster. You see, this is the main express," Jonathan said.

"How could it go any faster than the one we were on?" Celia gasped.

"Trust me and get prepared because it can," Jonathan warned.

"Well, I'm glad we still have civilized trains back home," Mandie remarked as she looked out the window and saw the train they had been on being readied to return to Paris. "Look what they're doing." She pointed.

Celia and Jonathan watched through the window with her as the engine from the other train was being disconnected and then run on a separate track that circled back onto the main track where it was coupled to the last car.

As the engine began to pull forward, Mandie remarked, "You know, all the people will have to ride backwards now, because all the seats faced forward when we were on it and they didn't turn the cars around!"

"No, most of the seats are reversible," Jonathan explained. "The conductor will just go through and flip all the seats to face the other direction. That is, except for the compartments like the one we were in. If you remember, those seats faced each other. Your grandmother and the senator rode facing backwards all the way."

"That's right," Mandie remembered.

Their train suddenly blew its whistle and took off with a jolt down the tracks. The young people still weren't expecting such a sudden movement and they grasped the arms of the seats to keep from being hurled to the floor.

There was no possibility of carrying on a normal conversation above the noise of the train. And it was going so fast Mandie was sure they would have a wreck any minute. Besides that, she had trouble on her hands in the form of a white kitten. Snowball definitely didn't like the fast ride and he clung frantically to Mandie's dress, meowing loudly in protest. Mandie tried to comfort the kitten and at the same time control her own fear of the fast-moving train.

When they finally arrived at the station in Rome, Italy, Mandie gave a sigh of relief as the train lunged to a halt.

"Thank the Lord we made it in one piece," Mandie gasped as she cuddled Snowball.

Mrs. Taft and the senator rose. "Now, everyone stay close together. This is a busy place and it would be easy to get lost," Mrs. Taft warned the young people.

The senator stepped down and helped Mrs. Taft from the train. The young people followed. Mandie and Celia stared about them.

"So this is the capital of Italy," Mandie remarked, holding her pet securely. "Remember when we studied the Roman Empire, Celia? Just look at all the beautiful architecture," she said, indicating their surroundings in the huge, magnificent train station.

"And it's so old and full of history," Celia added.

"So much history that even a person who was born here doesn't know all of it," Jonathan said.

Mrs. Taft stopped to look back at them. "Amanda, Celia, and Jonathan," she called, "hurry up. Senator Morton will hire a carriage to take us to our hotel."

Mandie and Celia were so fascinated by the architecture overhead and the old statues in the depot, they kept bumping into people.

Jonathan made sure that they kept in sight of the adults. Otherwise they all would have been lost. "You girls think this building is something? Just wait till you see the Colosseum and the Sistine Chapel and the Pantheon and the Forum and the hundreds—probably thousands—of fountains here in Italy," he told them.

"I'm so excited. I don't want to waste a minute," Mandie replied, hurrying to catch up with the adults. As she did, a woman came bursting around a corner in the corridor, and Mandie had to jump aside to keep from running into her. Then as she disappeared just as quickly into the crowd, Mandie stopped suddenly, causing Celia and Jonathan to bump into her. "That woman!" Mandie exclaimed. "That was the strange woman from the ship!" She pointed in the direction she had disappeared.

"Are you sure, Mandie?" Celia asked.

"Of course, I'm sure, Celia," Mandie said sharply. "As much as we've seen that woman, I know her when I see her."

"Well, it's too late to catch up with her now," Jonathan told the girls. "Come on, Mandie. Your grandmother is getting ahead of us."

There had been a strange woman on board the ship they had sailed on to England, and she seemed to follow the girls everywhere they went. Then they had seen the same woman in London, and she had turned up again in Paris. But she always vanished before they could catch up with her.

Mandie stomped her foot. "I am going to find out who that woman is if it's the last thing I do," she said.

"Mandie, that woman is dangerous," Celia told her as they hurried on through the depot. "You know what happened to us in Paris. I think we ought to stay as far away from that woman as possible."

"But she's not staying away from us!" Mandie reminded her friend.

"I wouldn't pay any attention to her if I were you. You know now not to trust strangers," Jonathan said.

"I wouldn't pay attention to her if she'd just stop following us around everywhere we go," Mandie replied.

They followed the adults into a waiting room.

Mrs. Taft turned to them and said, "Sit down right there," indicating a bench across the room. "Senator Morton will get us a carriage."

The senator went through the revolving doors, and the young people sat down.

"I don't think we should tell my grandmother about my seeing that strange woman," Mandie said under her breath as Mrs. Taft stood just inside the doorway across the room. "It would just worry her."

"All right, Mandie," Celia agreed. "But if that woman does anything besides follow us around, we'll have to tell your grandmother."

"Agreed," Mandie replied, holding on to Snowball.

"I'll help you watch out for her," Jonathan offered.

"Well, I hope we don't see her again," Mandie said.

Senator Morton came back inside to show them to the waiting carriage. The young people followed the adults outside. Mandie and Celia again stopped to stare. The city was so old and beautiful. The girls had never seen anything like the huge structures about them.

"Amanda, Celia," Mrs. Taft called from the carriage. "Come along. We'll go sightseeing later. Right now we've got to get to the hotel."

The hotel wasn't far away, and the short journey in the carriage was so exciting the girls wished it could last longer. Jonathan and the adults pointed out several famous landmarks along the way.

"Oh, Grandmother, I wish we could stay here the rest of the year," Mandie said. "We'll never be able to see it all on such a short visit."

"Don't worry, dear. We'll manage to fit it all in," Mrs. Taft assured her.

The carriage came to a stop before a magnificent hotel. Mandie's blue eyes grew big. "Are we staying in this place?" she asked.

"Yes, dear," Mrs. Taft replied, stepping down from the carriage. "Now you young people stay right with me while the senator checks us in." She led the way into the lobby.

Senator Morton went to the front desk, and Mrs. Taft sat down on a nearby settee. The young people walked around the lobby to inspect their surroundings. The walls and floor were shiny marble, and there were paintings on the tile ceiling overhead. Roman statues stood as if in attendance, and the artwork of famous artists graced the walls.

Mandie gazed about in awe. "This must be an awfully rich country!" she remarked.

"Not really, Mandie," Jonathan said. "Your grandmother just stays in the best hotels. I'm afraid we haven't really seen how the average European lives."

"You're probably right," Mandie admitted. "But I do know how poor people live, because I was poor once myself, that is before I found my Uncle John and my real mother. And my Cherokee kinpeople are poor compared to most white people." Turning to look into Jonathan's dark eyes, she added, "But you probably don't know much about being poor since your father is so rich."

"I've never really been poor myself, but I do know how poor people live," Jonathan told her. "In most of the private schools my father has sent me to, we have adopted a poor family and helped them to live more comfortably."

"That's what we do back home in Virginia," Celia said. "All the people in our neighborhood try to help poor farmers who don't have much."

Senator Morton rejoined Mrs. Taft and she beckoned to the young people, "We're ready to go to our rooms, dears."

The three young people followed the adults down a huge corridor to an elevator, which they had learned early in their travels was called a lift in Europe.

"A lift?" Mandie complained, holding her stomach.

Jonathan smiled. "At least this one has a glass door, so you can see what we're passing on the way up."

"That doesn't help much. I don't like them," Mandie said.

Celia sighed. "Me either. They make my stomach turn over."

The elevator doors opened, and the girls reluctantly stepped inside behind the adults, Jonathan entering last. They all turned to face the front as the operator slid the door shut. Mandie and Celia held hands and closed their eyes as the elevator began ascending. Snowball squirmed restlessly in Mandie's other arm.

A few moments later, it came to a halt, and the door opened.

"Here we are," Senator Morton announced.

As they entered the empty hallway, Mandie looked

around. "I certainly hope that strange woman doesn't follow us here," Mandie whispered to her friends. "I want to enjoy this city."

Noticing their whispered conversation, Mrs. Taft said, "I do hope you young people are not planning secrets again."

"No, ma'am," the three chimed. They looked at each other and smiled.

We aren't planning secrets, Mandie thought. *We just don't want to be followed around by that woman.*

Chapter 2 / The Magician

When they reached their suites, they found the doors standing open, and a young man in uniform waiting to assist them in any way he could. He explained in broken English where he had placed their bags. The senator and Jonathan shared a suite across the hall from the others.

"Thank you," Mrs. Taft said to the man as she and the girls went inside.

Mandie saw that the girls' belongings were all together in the larger bedroom, and Mrs. Taft's were in the other. She wondered how the man knew what belonged to whom and which room each would have. Then she remembered they had name tags on all their luggage.

Mandie smiled at the dark-haired man.

The bellhop noticed Snowball in Mandie's arms and motioned for Mandie to follow him to the other side of the parlor. There he pointed to a sandbox for the kitten. Mandie set Snowball down, and the kitten immediately explored the box.

When the man started to leave, Mandie said, "Thank you."

"*Prego*," the bellhop replied, motioning with his

hands. "Welcome." He left the room to cross the hall to the senator's suite.

Mandie stopped Jonathan, who was still in the hallway. "Where can we buy those bags to carry our journals in?" she asked.

"There are shops in this hotel," Jonathan replied. "We can probably find some there."

"Could we get them now?" Mandie asked as Celia came to the doorway.

"Ask your grandmother," Jonathan answered.

Mandie rushed back into the suite to get permission from her grandmother, who gave Mandie strict instructions that she and her friends were not to go anywhere but the shops and should not be gone long.

"Come on, Celia," Mandie said. Leaving Snowball to continue exploring the room, she closed the door.

"Do you have money, Mandie?" Celia asked.

"Oh, no!" Mandie exclaimed. "We don't have any Italian money."

"Oh, that's right!" Celia remembered. "I have some English and French money, besides a few American dollars."

"Come on," Jonathan called from the doorway of the parlor. "We can exchange it at the front desk, like we did in France."

The tall, elderly man on duty in the lobby spoke perfect English but had a little trouble understanding *American* English. But when the girls began pulling dollars out of their bags, he understood their intentions.

"We want to use our money in your shops," Mandie told the man.

"Dollars?" the man questioned.

"*Lire*," Jonathan said. "We need lire for our dollars."

"Sí, sí. Yes, lire for dollars," the man said. Taking the girls' money from the counter, he turned to open the safe behind him. "Shops are one floor down," he said over his shoulder.

"We are so anxious to see everything!" Mandie enthused. "I think we're going to the Colosseum and the Roman Forum and the Capitol, and all those wonderful places you have here in your city."

The man turned back with a handful of lire and began counting the money into the girls' hands. When he finished, he looked up and said, "Don't forget the catacombs."

"Oh, we wouldn't miss seeing them," Mandie assured him.

"Good. The catacombs are the ancient underground cemeteries of the Christians," the man explained. "There are several, but the ones most visited are the Catacombs of St. Sebastian. A basilica was built over these in the fourth century in honor of the apostles Peter and Paul."

"They're that old?" Mandie asked.

The man nodded.

"And we can go under the ground and see them?" Celia questioned.

"Yes, all the catacombs are open to the public," the man replied. "The Franciscans are the custodians of St. Sebastian's, and of course the blessed St. Sebastian himself is buried there."

"I've never been to the catacombs," Jonathan said. "Can we actually walk around down there?"

"Of course," the clerk replied. "You will find several rooms, or sections, and a maze of passageways to explore."

"And there are graves there?" Mandie asked.

"Actually, they are what we call crypts nowadays," the clerk explained. Noticing another customer standing at the counter, he told Mandie and her friends, "We hope you enjoy your visit in our city. If we can be of any assistance to you, please inform us." He smiled and turned to his other customer.

Mandie glanced at the tall, well-dressed young man with thick blond hair and deep blue eyes. He caught her looking at him and quickly turned his back and leaned on the counter.

Celia and Jonathan started walking toward the elevator. "Come on, Mandie," Celia called.

Mandie caught up with her friends. "Did y'all see that handsome man back there at the counter?" she asked. "He looked like someone important."

"Humph! He looked like a plain old actor to me," Jonathan said. "Like the ones we have in New York."

"An actor?" Celia said brightly. She stopped to look back. "I think actors are such interesting people."

"I do, too," Mandie agreed.

While the young people waited for the elevator to descend so they could take it to the lower level, Mandie looked back down the hallway. The tall man was going into a room about halfway down the corridor.

"Look!" she said, glancing in his direction. "There he is."

"He went into that room," Celia added.

"So he must be staying in this hotel," Jonathan said.

The elevator arrived, and the girls reluctantly entered and held hands as it moved down to another floor. When it stopped, they rushed out into the hallway and looked down the corridors, which were so long they seemed to vanish from sight. There were shops of all sorts, covering every inch of space.

"Look at all the stores!" Celia exclaimed.

Mandie and her friends walked down the crowded corridor. "We ought to be able to find those mesh bags in one of these places, Jonathan," she said.

"Remember, your grandmother said we had to hurry back," Celia reminded her.

"It won't take long to find a bag," Jonathan assured them. "Let's go in this shop here," he said, pointing to the first one on the right.

The girls followed him into the open storefront. There were scarves, jewelry, and trinkets of every kind displayed on the counters.

Mandie and Celia were so fascinated with the colorful array that they would have looked at each item if Jonathan hadn't asked the proprietor if he sold the mesh bags they were looking for.

The man understood English and immediately pulled a handful of bags out from under the counter and laid them out for the girls to see.

"You mean those are bags?" Mandie asked Jonathan as she examined the tangled mess of brightly colored twine.

Jonathan picked one up and stretched it out. As the girls watched, it became a full-sized bag.

"There, you see? You can fold it up when you're not using it and put it in your purse," he told the girls.

"Oh, I like these!" Mandie exclaimed. She picked up a red one, stretching it as she had seen Jonathan do.

"So do I," Celia agreed, choosing a green one.

"Are you going to buy them?" Jonathan asked.

"Oh, yes," Mandie replied. "I want this red one. It'll match Snowball's leash and harness."

"And I'll take this green one," Celia said, giggling. "It'll match my eyes."

The girls began pulling money out of their bags to pay the shopkeeper.

"Jonathan, I know you didn't bring any money," Mandie said. "If you want one of these, I'll buy one for you."

Jonathan blushed. "No, no, Mandie. Men don't carry those things. They're only for ladies."

"I could loan you some money if there's something else you'd like to buy," Celia offered.

"Thanks, but I don't know of anything," Jonathan replied. "Besides, the senator has offered to loan me money until my father comes."

The girls handed the proprietor some lire, and Jonathan watched as the man counted their change.

Mandie stuffed the change into her purse as she held the bright new bag. "I hope your father doesn't come for you," she told Jonathan.

"I don't think he will. He's always too occupied with all his business," Jonathan replied as they left the shop.

Mandie led the way toward the elevator and suddenly stopped. "Look! There are some steps. Let's walk up."

"You mean all the way to the fourth floor?" Celia asked.

"Why not?" Jonathan said, going toward the wide marble steps.

"Come on," Mandie urged Celia. She followed Jonathan, and Celia reluctantly joined them.

They started up enthusiastically, but by the time they reached the fourth floor, they were all out of breath.

Mandie wiped her brow with her handkerchief. "I don't know which is worse—the steps or the lift."

"The steps," Celia said, breathlessly.

Jonathan laughed and plopped down on the top step. "You girls haven't been getting enough exercise," he teased.

"Look who's talking!" Mandie exclaimed. "I could probably outwalk you any day, Jonathan Guyer."

"Oh, I doubt that," Jonathan said with his impish smile.

"Don't forget, Mandie's one-fourth Cherokee," Celia reminded him.

"What's that got to do with it?" Jonathan asked.

Mandie and Celia sat down beside him. "Indians are great walkers," Mandie told him. She tried to push loose strands of her blond hair back under her bonnet. "Besides, I was raised in the country, and I also visit my Cherokee kinpeople a lot."

"I'd like to visit them," Jonathan said. "I've never seen a real Indian, except for your friend, Uncle Ned."

"Maybe you can come visit sometime," Mandie suggested. "Uncle Ned's wife, Morning Star, can't speak much English, but their granddaughter Sally lives with them, and she is as educated as we are."

"After Mandie's father died, her Uncle John married Mandie's mother," Celia explained. "He's one-half Cherokee, and he looks more Indian than Mandie does."

"My father's people are all of Dutch ancestry," Jonathan said.

"And what about your mother's people?" Mandie asked.

"I don't really know. I never thought about it because my mother died when I was a baby." Jonathan stood up. "Let's go."

They hurried down the corridor and quickly found their rooms. Mandie and Celia entered their parlor, and

Jonathan went into his suite across the hall.

Looking around, the girls found that the suite was empty. "Well, where's Grandmother?" Mandie fussed. "She told us to hurry back, and she's gone when we return." She peeked into the girls' bedroom and saw Snowball curled up on their big bed sound asleep.

"Let's see if she's across the hall," Celia said, going to open the door.

At that same moment, Jonathan came out of his suite. "No one's here," he said as the girls appeared in the doorway.

"Here either," Mandie replied. "I wonder where my grandmother and the senator could have gone. It seems odd that they would go off and leave us."

"I suppose we could get cleaned up while we wait," Celia suggested.

"Maybe they'll be back by that time," Mandie agreed.

"Right," Jonathan replied. "See you girls later," he said, going back inside and closing the door.

The girls returned to their bedroom. Their clothes were hung in the huge wardrobe, evidently unpacked by the maid. They chose fresh dresses and laid them out. Then they took turns taking baths in the huge marble tub in the adjoining bathroom. They brushed out their long hair and pinned it back up on top of their heads.

Mandie unbuttoned the red voile dress she had chosen and carefully stepped into it. "Goodness, you'd think Grandmother would be back by now," she said.

Celia fastened the neck of her bright yellow dress. "Mandie, do you think we were gone too long and they went looking for us?" she asked.

Mandie thought for a moment. "No, I don't think so. We weren't gone that long."

"I sure hope they weren't worried," Celia said.

"Do you suppose we should go looking for them?" Mandie asked, twirling her long skirt before the floor-length mirror on the wall.

"Oh, no," Celia said. "They might come back and we'd be gone."

Mandie sat on the bed. "This is getting to be a habit, you know," she said. "Remember? When we were in the hotel in Paris, Jonathan went off and didn't come back. I'm beginning to dislike hotel rooms."

"They'll probably be back any minute," Celia answered, shaking out the gathers in her skirt.

"Let's see if Jonathan is ready yet," Mandie suggested, going toward the door.

Celia followed her friend.

Mandie opened the door and gasped. "Quick! That strange woman was standing outside our door!" Mandie exclaimed, rushing into the corridor. "She went that way. Let's find her!"

"Mandie!" Celia cried, grabbing Mandie's arm. "Suppose your grandmother comes back while we're looking for that woman?"

Mandie turned back and sighed. "You're right, Celia. Oh, well, she must be staying in this hotel. We'll just have to catch up with her later. Let's see if Jonathan is ready." She crossed the hall and knocked lightly on the door to the senator's suite.

Jonathan opened the door, dressed in stylish new clothes. "Are they back yet?" he asked.

"No. We were about to ask you the same thing," Mandie told him. "But, Jonathan, guess what? I just saw that strange woman from the ship again. She was standing right outside our door when I opened it."

"Did you ask her what she wanted?" he inquired.

"No, she was too quick for me. She disappeared down that way," Mandie said, pointing down the hallway.

"You know, I'd really like to know who that woman is," Jonathan said.

At that moment Mrs. Taft and Senator Morton came rushing down the hallway toward them.

"Oh, dears, I'm sorry we've been gone so long," Mrs. Taft said. "I thought we'd get back before y'all did or we wouldn't have gone. But it was so exciting!"

"Grandmother, what?" Mandie asked.

Mrs. Taft stopped to catch her breath. "We were invited to tea," she explained after a moment. "That famous English actor, George Rushton, was the guest of honor. You see, I have some old friends staying here, and they know him personally. He was—"

"Grandmother," Mandie interrupted as the girls looked at each other, "what does this actor look like?"

"He's very handsome—tall, blond hair," her grandmother replied. "Young and—" She started to enter their suite.

"And deep blue eyes, darker blue than mine," Mandie added.

Mrs. Taft turned around and looked at the girls. "Why, yes, dear. How did you know?" she asked.

"We saw him in the lobby," Mandie said. To Jonathan she added, "You were right. He is an actor!"

"I was only guessing," Jonathan said. "It might not be the same person."

"He's some sort of magician, too, between his regular stage plays," Mrs. Taft explained. "Anyway, let me get dressed for dinner. I'm glad to see you girls are ready. We'll be with you shortly, Senator," she said as he and Jonathan went to their suite.

Mrs. Taft started toward her bedroom, then stopped. "Amanda, would you please unhook this necklace for me?" she asked. "I had a terrible time getting it fastened when I put it on." She touched the ruby-encrusted necklace around her neck and sat down on the settee so Mandie could reach the clasp.

It took Mandie several tries, but she finally succeeded in unhooking the necklace.

"Thanks, dear," her grandmother said, going on into her bedroom.

The girls sat talking on the settee in the parlor while Mrs. Taft got dressed.

"I'm sure he's the same man we saw in the lobby," Mandie said. "And Grandmother said he was also a magician. I'd like to see what magic tricks he can do."

"I would, too," Celia agreed.

"We'll have to ask Grandmother if he's performing here in Rome. If so, we'll just go see him," Mandie decided.

Chapter 3 / The Unseen Snuffer

Mandie and her friends stared at their beautiful surroundings that night as they waited behind Senator Morton and Mrs. Taft at the entrance to the hotel dining room. The white marble floor shone like a looking-glass. Supporting columns throughout the huge room were made of matching white tiles, and even the ceiling was inlaid with mosaics of various historical Italian figures.

Plush red draperies with gold tassels and fringe adorned the floor-length arched windows around the room. Massive carved chairs and tables stood across the space before them. Although huge crystal chandeliers full of gas lights hung from high above, there were candles on all the tables, and white tablecloths and napkins. Large vases of bright-colored flowers stood about the room amid the huge statues. Smaller containers of flowers graced each table.

"What a place!" Mandie whispered to her friends.

"Look at all the ladies," Celia said. "They look like they've just stepped out of a fashion boutique."

Jonathan smiled and said, "Don't forget the gentlemen. They certainly look fashionable, too."

Mandie turned and looked at Jonathan. "You know, so do you," she said. "I don't see how you manage to have such nice clothes with only that little bag you had when we found you on the ship."

"That's easy," Jonathan said, shrugging his broad shoulders. "Senator Morton was nice enough to loan me some money for clothes, and I went shopping while you and Celia were dressing for dinner tonight."

"You went shopping in that length of time?" Mandie asked.

"Why, yes, I went downstairs to some of the shops we saw this afternoon," the boy explained.

The head waiter led them to a table near a window where they could look out onto the street.

Mandie and Celia were more interested in watching the people outside the window than in ordering food.

"Girls, please," Mrs. Taft scolded. "We have to order our food." Turning to the senator, she added, "Sitting by this window was not such a good idea after all."

"I'm sure they'll eat when the food comes," Senator Morton assured her.

After they ordered, the waiter brought a basketful of breadsticks and butter, and the young people eagerly devoured them.

Mandie turned to look across the vast room. Spotting the blond man they had seen at the desk, she leaned forward to speak to her grandmother. "Look over there at the table near that post," she said, rolling her eyes in that direction. "That's the man we saw. Is he the same one you said is an actor?"

Mrs. Taft looked over at the man and then smiled at the young people. "One and the same," she said.

The waiter brought their food, and after returning

thanks, they all began eating.

"Is he putting on any magic acts while he's here in Rome?" Mandie asked.

"Why, yes. The play he was performing in has closed," Mrs. Taft replied. "In fact, I was going to ask if you young people would like to see his magic show. He's using a small theater within walking distance from here."

"Oh, yes!" the three said together.

"Could we go tonight, Grandmother?" Mandie asked excitedly.

"No, dear, by the time we finish our dinner it will be late, and we need some rest tonight," Mrs Taft told her. "What about tomorrow night?"

Mandie looked at her friends and they both nodded.

"Then we'll just go see this young man do his magic tricks tomorrow night," Senator Morton said. "I'll get the tickets."

"Thank you, Senator," Mrs. Taft smiled. Turning back to the young people, she said, "Senator Morton and I thought perhaps y'all would like to begin your sightseeing tomorrow with a tour of the catacombs, and then maybe the Colosseum and the other ruins here in Rome."

"Oh, the catacombs would be great!" Mandie exclaimed.

"Yes, I think they would be very interesting," Jonathan agreed.

"Well, I suppose we'll have to see them sometime or other, but I'm not very anxious to visit dead people," Celia said hesitantly.

Mandie and Jonathan laughed. The adults smiled.

"I'll stay right with you, Celia, I promise," Mandie said solemnly.

"So will I," Jonathan added.

"Celia, dear, if you'd rather not go inside, I believe there's a little refreshment stand at the entrance where you can wait," Mrs. Taft suggested.

"Oh, no," Celia quickly objected. "I'll have to go inside. You see, I have to keep up with my journal, and I'd hate to write in it that I was there and didn't go inside."

When they had all finished eating, Mandie asked the waiter for some food to take to her kitten. She had locked Snowball in their bathroom and brought the key with her.

Snowball was curled up asleep in the middle of the huge marble bathtub when Mandie opened the door. Seeing his mistress, he stood up, stretched, and yawned.

"Here," Mandie said to him, holding out the saucer of food she had brought. "Here's your dinner, Snowball."

Sniffing the aroma of food, Snowball jumped out of the bathtub and rushed to his mistress. Mandie placed the saucer and a cup of water in a corner for him. He quickly devoured it all.

Putting the key back in the bathroom door lock, Mandie went in to the bedroom and got ready for bed. "This was a lot easier than trying to tie Snowball under the table or somewhere while we ate," she told Celia.

"As long as the maid doesn't have a duplicate key. . . ." Celia answered, getting into her nightgown and robe. "She might accidentally let him out."

"Oh, I hadn't thought of that," Mandie said. "Well, I'll just take him with us tomorrow. He's pretty good about walking with his leash and harness on now."

"I'll help you with him," Celia promised.

It was warm in the room, and the girls pulled back some of the heavy draperies looking for a window they could open. To their surprise they found a French door behind one of the curtains.

Mandie pressed her face against the glass and peered out. "Well, we have a door," she said. "Hey, Celia, look, there are steps outside that go down."

Celia looked over Mandie's shoulder. "They must lead to the street."

"It looks that way," Mandie said.

Celia continued peering through the glass. "There's a balcony out there, too."

Mandie tried to turn the doorknob. "It's locked," she said, noticing a large key in the lock. "Should we unlock it and open the door a bit for some air?"

"Oh, no, no," Celia protested. "Please don't, Mandie. It's so dark. Someone could be outside."

Mandie laughed. "All right. When it's daylight I'll open it and look outside." She turned toward the window they had uncovered. "If you'll help me, I think we can push this window up so we can get some air."

The window was huge, and it took the strength of both girls to raise it. A cool breeze immediately floated into their room.

"Mmmm!" Mandie breathed in. "It was worth all the trouble, wasn't it?"

Celia looked outside. There was nothing there but another wall of the hotel. "I suppose so ... as long as someone can't get in." She walked over to the French door. "But we've got to cover this door. Somebody might look in while we're asleep." She pulled the curtains shut.

The girls hopped into the big bed, and Snowball pounced on their feet. With the window open, they could hear a lot of noise from the outside. Someone was singing opera in loud, high notes, and someone else was playing an accordion. The buzz of conversation on the street below sounded like a hundred people talking in loud tones all at once.

"This sure is different from home, where everything is quiet and you can hear the jarflies at night, isn't it?" Mandie said. She wiggled around in an effort to dislodge Snowball, who had curled up on her feet. "Snowball, I didn't need you to heat up my feet." She reached down to push him to one side.

Snowball meowed and gradually inched his way back toward her feet.

The girls were tired from the long journey from France, but they were wide awake with the excitement of being in Rome. They talked into the wee hours of the morning.

When the maid came in at dawn and pulled back the draperies, Mandie and Celia had trouble getting their eyes all the way open.

Mandie rubbed her eyelids as she sat up. "Feels like dirt in my eyes."

"*Buon giorno, signorina*," the maid said as Mandie swung her feet out of the bed. The girl had brought a breakfast tray, and she placed it on a table nearby.

"Sorry, I don't understand Italian," Mandie apologized as she smiled at the heavy-set young girl.

"I only said, good morning, miss," the maid translated. "Would you like me to pour out coffee?"

"Oh, you speak English, thank goodness," Mandie said, standing up and stretching. Celia joined her by the table. "Pour out the coffee? No, we don't want it poured out. We'll drink it."

"Then I go." The girl smiled as she left the room.

"Mandie, I think she meant pour it out into our cups," Celia explained. "My mother has some friends back home who came from England, and that's the way they say it."

"Well, I'm glad you understand these things," Mandie said, laughing.

As soon as everyone had enjoyed a light breakfast in their rooms, Mrs. Taft and Senator Morton took the young people sightseeing.

It was a bright, clear day and warm. As they rode down the cobblestone streets of Rome in a hired carriage, the girls were overwhelmed by the huge stone buildings, the grassy parks with fountains everywhere they looked, and the crowds of people on the streets, who all seemed to be talking loudly and gesturing with their hands. Mandie and Celia, who were both country girls, had never seen such a bustling, interesting city.

Mrs. Taft laid out their plans. "We'll go to the catacombs first," she said. "Then we'll have something to eat at noon and go on to some of the ruins, or the Colosseum."

"Yes, let's go to the catacombs first and get that over with," Celia remarked, patting the mesh bag in her lap that contained her journal.

"And write in our journals about it?" Mandie asked. She had the harness and leash on Snowball, who sat purring at her side.

"Yes, that will be something to write about," Celia agreed.

At the entrance to the Catacombs of St. Sebastian a Franciscan monk greeted them together with lots of other visitors. He wore a long, brown hooded robe, and had leather sandals on his feet. He gave a brief explanation of the tour in several different languages.

"If you will please follow me," he said, "we will enter the basilica here. It was built in the fourth century in honor of the Apostles Peter and Paul." He led the way inside the rectangular building, which contained two aisles amid rows of huge columns and a nave.

Celia held on to Mandie's hand as they followed the others.

"Over here—" the monk said, indicating a huge archway, "—you will find the entrance to the underground catacombs." Then he gestured toward the display cases along the walls. "Inside these cases you will see some of the precious gems of our country. These and other artifacts here were found in ruins that have only recently been uncovered."

Everyone crowded around the thick glass-covered displays to gaze at the arrangements of sparkling gems and artifacts of gold and silver.

Mandie gasped. "Oh, they're beautiful! Look at that huge ruby in the center of this piece. I've never seen anything like it before."

"Neither have I," Celia said in wonder.

Jonathan smiled at their enthusiasm.

Mrs. Taft and Senator Morton led the way, and Mandie held Snowball tightly as she and Celia and Jonathan descended the stairs. They soon found themselves in an underground cavern lit only by candles, and having a damp odor. The visitors were silent in reverence for the Christians buried there. The walls were rough stone, and crevices in the wall held small crypts containing the remains of the dead.

Celia began shaking, and she grabbed on to Mandie's hand.

"Celia," Mandie said, "Jonathan and I are right here with you. There is nothing to be afraid of. Dead people can't hurt you," she tried to reassure her friend.

"I know," Celia replied in a quivering voice. "I'm sorry

to be such a scaredy-cat, but the very thought of people buried here gives me the jitters." She laughed nervously.

There were several archways leading into the various sections of the catacombs. The crowd had thinned out after a quick look, and Mrs. Taft and Senator Morton became engrossed with carved tablets in the walls, which they tried to decipher.

Jonathan led the girls forward. "Here's another room over here," he said. "Look!" He stepped through an archway into a corridor that went around a bend, and the girls followed.

Mandie freed her hand from Celia's long enough to push her bonnet back so she could see better. The long ribbon secured it on her neck. Celia pushed hers back too.

"I don't know whether it's hot or cold down here," Mandie remarked, breaking the silence. "I feel hot, but the air around us feels cold."

The young people looked around the room for some connecting corridor.

"This seems to be a dead end," Mandie said.

"You're right," Jonathan agreed. "But look at this carving on the wall."

The three inspected the ancient writing, barely visible from the light of only one candle near the archway they had come through.

"Is it Latin, Jonathan?" Mandie asked, pointing to the inscription.

Jonathan bent to look closer. At that moment the candle went out. Jonathan caught his breath. The girls grabbed each other. The three were left in complete darkness. The bend in the corridor kept light from coming in from other rooms.

"Where is everybody?" Mandie cried. "I can't hear a sound."

There was not a single noise to indicate that anyone else remained in the underground caverns.

Jonathan began feeling his way along the wall. "I think I can locate the archway that we came through," he said. "You girls hold on to my coat."

Mandie and Celia took hold of his coattail and followed him closely in the blackness.

"Wh-what do you suppose made the candle go out?" Celia stammered.

"There must have been a draft down here," Jonathan said, moving along in small, careful steps. "Let's see, I believe I've found the entrance." He moved a little more and said, "Yes, I think this is where we came in. Now, stay close together."

He stepped cautiously through the archway. It was still completely dark in the corridor.

"Jonathan, what happened to the candles that were along the way when we came in here?" Mandie asked, holding tightly to her kitten.

"They all seem to have gone out," Jonathan said, still moving slowly as he felt his way along the stone wall.

"Then someone must have put them out," Mandie reasoned. "I don't see how a little draft could blow them all out at once."

"Oh, no!" Celia moaned.

"Don't panic," Jonathan told the girls. "We'll be out of here in no time, and then we'll find out what happened."

"Why don't we call out for help?" Celia asked.

"Too embarrassing," Jonathan said, as he kept inching his way along. "Don't worry. We'll be out of here soon."

As they moved along at a snail's pace, Jonathan suddenly cried out. "Ouch!" He stood still.

"What's wrong?" Mandie asked.

"Nothing. I must have put my hand right on top of a candle that just went out. The wax was hot," he explained.

They moved along through what seemed to be several rooms, and still no light appeared anywhere. The girls were getting frantic. Every time they whispered, their voices echoed back at them.

"Jonathan, someone has put out all the candles, or we would have found a lighted one by now," Mandie complained, nervously clutching Snowball.

"It sure looks that way," Jonathan admitted. "But if we keep going, we're bound to find the entrance. Then we can get out of this place."

"I don't understand why we keep moving and still don't find anyone else down here," Mandie said shakily. "Where is my grandmother . . . and the senator?"

Jonathan kept feeling his way along with the girls closely following, but they didn't find a single light or another person anywhere.

"We must have made a wrong turn somewhere," Mandie decided. "I don't know how we're ever going to get out of here. We seem to be going deeper and deeper inside these caverns."

Jonathan sighed. "You may be right, Mandie," he said.

Chapter 4 / Lost in the Dark

"Jonathan, I'm getting tired," Mandie complained. "We must have walked a mile by now and haven't gotten anyplace." She and Celia were close behind him.

"My legs are getting so wobbly I can hardly stand up." Celia's voice quivered in fright.

"I'm sorry," Jonathan replied. Just then he stumbled on something and the girls almost fell because they were still holding on to his coattail. "I'm sorry again," he said. "My foot hit something rough and moveable, probably a stone."

"Do you think we could rest for a minute?" Mandie asked. "Snowball is squirming so. I'd like to set him down."

"All right. A minute would be the time it takes to count to sixty." Jonathan was apparently trying to joke, but his voice sounded nervous. "Hold on, now, so you don't fall. I'm going to stop here."

Mandie sighed heavily. "I don't understand how all this happened to us," she said.

"Neither do I," Jonathan replied. "I'm beginning to think someone deliberately blew out the candle in the room where we were."

"But all the other candles were out, too," Celia added in a shaky voice.

Mandie gasped. "Do y'all think someone is trying to trap us, or follow us?" She shivered at the thought.

"I certainly hope not," Jonathan said as the three huddled closer together in the dark cavern.

The thought of someone near them in the darkness made Mandie want to get out of there fast. "Maybe we'd better keep moving," she suggested. "Eventually, we've got to get somewhere."

"Okay, hold on to me and stay together," Jonathan replied. "I'm going to start walking again. Ready?"

"Yes," the girls replied together as Jonathan moved forward.

At that instant the ground seemed to open up beneath Jonathan's feet. He began falling into space. The girls fell with him, and Snowball clung to Mandie.

"Wow!" Jonathan hollered as he fell through the air. He landed below.

"Dear God, please help us!" Mandie cried. The girls clung to one another as they fell down beside Jonathan.

Mandie rubbed her painful bottom and looked around in the dim light. A monk in a hooded robe was crouching in the corner of the room they had fallen into. Mandie and Jonathan got up right away, but Celia remained on the floor, still shaken from the sudden fall.

Mandie walked cautiously toward the monk. "Please, mister, can you help us get out of this place?" she asked.

Snowball jumped up and raced about the room.

The man bowed his hood-covered head and backed quickly away from Mandie, apparently fearful of the sudden visitors from the floor above. He began chattering in frightened tones in another language.

"I'm sorry if we scared you," Mandie told the man. She tried get closer to him and see his face, but he kept his distance and his face concealed within the full hood of his robe.

Jonathan tried speaking to the tall, mysterious monk. "Could you please just tell us how to get out of here?" he asked him.

The monk continued backing away.

Mandie turned to her friend, who still sat on the floor. "Celia, are you all right?" She bent to look at her.

Celia reached up and Mandie helped her to stand. But Celia was still shaking. "I'm all right," she said in a hoarse whisper. She shook out her rumpled dress.

Mandie looked back at the monk. "Jonathan, try French," she begged. "Maybe he understands that language."

Jonathan did as she suggested. "We are sorry for disturbing you, but we are lost and are trying to get back outside. Can you help us?"

The monk continued to back away until he bumped into what looked like a concrete casket standing upright behind him. He turned, quickly pushed the lid aside and jumped in, closing the cover behind him.

Mandie gasped. "What on earth is he doing?"

They all stared after the monk, who had vanished into the standing vault.

Jonathan rushed forward and tried to move the lid. "Let's see if we can get this open," he said to the girls.

Mandie immediately went to help him.

Celia lagged behind. "Isn't that a c-c-casket?" she asked.

Jonathan smiled at her. "Whatever it is, there was

enough room inside for the man to get in. There can't be a body inside."

Celia shivered and then hesitantly touched the cold stone in an effort to help lift the lid.

"It's so heavy we can't even budge it, Jonathan," Mandie complained. They all grunted and groaned as they worked on the lid. "How did he ever open it so easily?" she asked.

"There must be a latch or something to release it," Jonathan replied. He bent to walk around the casket and examine the edges.

Mandie and Celia followed him. Snowball continued to race around the room.

"No luck." Mandie sighed. "If I hadn't seen the man open it and get inside, I'd say it was impossible."

Celia stayed close to Mandie. "Where are we anyway?" she asked, shivering in the damp, musty-smelling room.

"There isn't a door or opening anywhere to get out of here that I can see," Mandie remarked as she quickly walked around the small room. She stopped suddenly. "You know, there must be an exit in that casket! There's no other way out of here."

She looked up at the small, barred openings high in the wall on one side. "It would be impossible to get through one of those windows up there. They aren't large enough. So how did the man get in here? Not only that, how did we get in here?" She looked overhead. "Look, there's not even a hole in the ceiling where we fell through."

"A trap door!" Jonathan exclaimed, scanning the ceiling. "We accidentally stepped on a trap door, and when we fell through, it closed up again." He pointed above. "Look! See the cracks in the stone up there in the corner?

That's got to be where we fell through."

"You're right," Mandie agreed, following his gaze. "There's no way to get up there. Even if we could, we probably couldn't open the trap door." She looked around the room. There didn't seem to be a single thing in the place except for the casket.

"What can we do?" Celia moaned.

"Let's reenact what that monk did," Mandie suggested. "Jonathan, make like you're that man. He was standing right here when I first saw him." She pointed to a place near where she stood, and Jonathan came to stand there.

"Then he began backing away from us," Jonathan said as he started walking backwards.

"Toward the casket, Jonathan," Mandie reminded him.

Jonathan glanced behind him and moved back toward the coffin. Mandie followed slowly, with Celia hovering nearby. Since they were all looking at the floor in search of a release for the lid or something hidden that the monk might have used, Jonathan abruptly bumped into the casket behind him. Nothing happened.

Mandie sighed in exasperation. "The monk was able to get the lid open. Let's try again."

The three of them once again used every ounce of their strength to try to budge the concrete lid. They couldn't get it to even shake, much less move. They just stood there, looking at it.

"If we could only figure out the secret of opening that stubborn lid . . ." Mandie said.

"Maybe the man locked the lid from inside after he went through," Celia suggested.

Mandie and Jonathan immediately turned to her.

"You're probably right, Celia," Mandie agreed. "He locked the lid so we couldn't follow him."

Jonathan shook his head and looked around the small room. "But I don't understand why he would want to lock us up in here," he said. "Surely he knows we have to get out some way or other."

Celia shivered again. "Mandie, I'm awfully afraid."

Mandie turned to her friend and said, "Celia, we need to say our verse." She reached for Celia's and Jonathan's hands. "Ready?"

Her friends nodded and Mandie led the recitation of their favorite verse. "What time I am afraid I will put my trust in Thee."

The girls blew out a deep breath and Mandie said, "Now we have to trust in the Lord to help us."

"But don't you think we need to *help* the Lord help us?" Jonathan asked.

"Well, I don't think He expects us to just sit down and wait for Him to perform a miracle," Mandie agreed.

"Maybe if we yelled real loud, somebody would hear us," Celia suggested, staying close to Mandie.

"These walls are probably soundproof," Jonathan told her. "They look thick, and remember how the other rooms seemed to be so silent?"

"Well, I agree with Celia," Mandie said, stomping her foot. "Let's try it. When we count to three, let's all holler as loud as we can."

"All right," Celia agreed.

"All right," Jonathan relented. "But it isn't going to do any good."

"Ready? One . . . two . . . three," Mandie counted.

The three yelled at the top of their lungs. "Help! Help!" they cried. The sound reverberated off the stones and almost deafened them. They all clamped their hands over their ears.

Snowball was frightened by the noise and ran, meowing loudly, to his mistress. Mandie picked him up and tried to calm him as she whispered to him and rubbed his soft white fur.

"Snowball, I'm sorry," she told the kitten as she rubbed her cheek on his head. Snowball straightened up and ran his rough red tongue across her face.

When Mandie put Snowball down, he immediately ran across the room to one corner and stood there meowing. Mandie looked at him, puzzled.

"Snowball, you must want outside. I'm sorry but there's no door over there," she told the kitten.

"Maybe he thinks you can make one," Jonathan joked.

"I wish we could," Celia said.

Snowball suddenly yowled loudly and looked back at Mandie.

"My goodness, Snowball. That's enough to wake the dead!" Mandie exclaimed. Then she gasped, realizing what she had said. "Not the dead here in the catacombs, though," she said, laughing nervously. "Come here."

She walked toward him, and he continued wailing. As she stooped to pick him up, a piece of the stone wall suddenly swung open, knocking her to a sitting position on the rough floor. "Look!" she yelled to the others, pointing to the opening.

Jonathan and Celia quickly came across the room. Mandie grabbed her kitten and stood up.

Jonathan looked through the opening. "There are steps going up in there. Let's go!" he said excitedly.

As they moved toward the opening, a hooded, robed

figure coming down the stone steps blocked their way. All three young people froze. This couldn't be the same monk who disappeared from the room. He had been tall, and this man was short and fat.

When the monk saw them, he stopped and motioned for them to follow him. He babbled in a language they couldn't understand and turned to go back up the narrow, stone stairway.

Mandie and her friends looked at each other.

Mandie shrugged. "Well, it should be easy to find out where he wants us to go," Mandie said, quickly following the man up the steps.

"And anywhere would be better than here in this room," Celia added, joining her friend.

Jonathan brought up the rear. "I just wish I could understand what he's trying to tell us," he said in exasperation.

The steps seemed endless as the three hurried after the robed man. It was dark and musty smelling in the stairwell, and there were no openings along the way. A faint light from somewhere way above lighted the stairs enough to see the steps.

"Where do you suppose he is taking us?" Celia whispered to Mandie, staying close behind her friend.

Mandie held Snowball tightly. "I guess we'll find out soon," she replied.

"I hope it's soon," Jonathan added.

The man didn't stop babbling all the way up the steps. Finally the light grew brighter, and they suddenly found themselves outside in a garden full of brightly colored flowers and shrubbery. They shielded their eyes at the brightness and gazed around at the statues and fountains among the greenery.

"It's beautiful!" Mandie exclaimed. The monk spoke loudly to catch their attention. Then he pointed to their right and motioned for them to go that way.

Mandie got a better look at the man then and was surprised to see that he seemed to be awfully old and wrinkled in spite of his agility in climbing the dozens of steps. He caught her glance and gave her a big smile.

"Thank you," Mandie said, with her most winsome smile. The man didn't answer, but continued to point to their right and motioned for them to go ahead. Jonathan and Celia thanked him too, and the three started off in the direction that he indicated. Mandie glanced back in time to see the monk disappear down the steps.

They followed a stone pathway, and as they came around a bend they were amazed to find they were at the entrance to the catacombs.

"Well, how do you like that?" Mandie exclaimed, "Somehow we came through another exit."

Celia pushed back her tumbled auburn hair. "It must be awfully huge under there when you think how far we walked and everything," she commented.

"It is," Jonathan confirmed. "Remember, the guide said they were still excavating, so there's no telling how big the place actually is."

Visitors milled around the entrance as they approached. The three scanned the crowd for Mrs. Taft and Senator Morton.

"I don't see them anywhere, do y'all?" she asked.

"No," Celia replied.

"They're probably still inside," Jonathan remarked. "Come on." He led the way back inside the caverns, and they all kept watching for the adults.

Mandie finally spotted her grandmother and Senator Morton in practically the same spot she had last seen them. They were standing before a huge inscription on the stone wall. She turned to the others. "There they are," she said, motioning toward the adults. "What are we going to tell them?"

"The truth, Mandie," Celia said firmly.

Snowball was squirming to get down, and Mandie held him firmly. "But they'll never believe us," she protested. "And I'm not sure how long we've been gone, either."

"It doesn't really matter how long we've been gone," Jonathan said. "We'll have to tell them what happened, Mandie."

"I'll wait till Grandmother asks me, then I'll just answer her questions truthfully," Mandie decided. "Come on."

Mandie and her friends walked up to Mrs. Taft and the senator.

"Amanda, we were just going to look for y'all," Mrs. Taft said. "Are y'all ready to go?"

The young people looked at one another and smiled. Evidently they had not even been missed. In spite of the fact that the three looked dirty and rumpled, the adults didn't seem to notice.

Mandie quickly pulled her bonnet back into place and motioned for Celia to do the same. "We're ready, Grandmother," she replied.

Mrs. Taft finally turned and gave them her full attention. "This is such an interesting place I thought perhaps we could come back tomorrow or another day," she said. "The senator and I were delayed, trying to decipher the inscriptions, and I'm afraid we didn't get to see everything."

Senator Morton smiled. "And we decided it was time to get something to eat," he added.

"Sure, anything you say," Mandie quickly agreed, trying to hide her relief at not being missed. She put Snowball down to walk on his leash.

They worked their way through the crowd to the entrance, and once outside Senator Morton told them to wait on a bench in the front garden while he went to hire a carriage.

As they waited, Mrs. Taft asked, "Did y'all find the place interesting?"

•Mandie held on to the leash and let Snowball roam in the tall grass. "It was the most exciting place I've been to in a long time!" she exclaimed.

"Yes, ma'am," Celia added.

"I thought it was very educational," Jonathan remarked. "Something I won't forget for some time."

"That's good," Mrs. Taft replied. "Then I know you'll enjoy coming back."

The three young people rolled their eyes at one another when Mrs. Taft glanced away.

Suddenly Snowball pounced, and Mandie wasn't holding his leash tight enough. He managed to jerk loose and went running across the garden.

Mandie quickly chased him. "Snowball Shaw! You come back here! Right now!" she commanded, as she followed him past a group of people sitting on a wall.

The leash was trailing after him in the grass, and Mandie got close enough to step on the end of it. The kitten jerked to a halt. He looked back at his mistress and meowed meekly.

Mandie stooped and picked him up, wrapping the end of the leash around her wrist. As she straightened up, she looked directly into the face of the strange woman from the ship. Mandie gasped and started toward her. The woman quickly disappeared in the crowd.

Mandie stood there, frustrated. She scanned the people in the park. There were so many people around, it was hard to see very far. She stomped her foot and turned to go back to her friends.

"One of these days I'll catch up with you!" Mandie muttered under her breath as she walked back.

Mrs. Taft stood up. The senator had secured a carriage, and they were ready to go.

Mandie looked at Jonathan and Celia, and they all followed the adults.

"That strange woman was in the garden back there," Mandie told her friends in a whisper. "She got away like usual."

Jonathan shook his head. "We'll catch her one day," he promised in a low voice.

"But right now we've got to worry about coming back to this terrible place," Celia moaned.

"Maybe we'll find more secret places," Mandie teased as they boarded the carriage.

Chapter 5 / All About Rome

The sidewalk cafe where Senator Morton took the group for the midday meal was different from the ones in Paris.

The tables and chairs were larger, and about half of them were set outside on the marble sidewalk while the other half were under cover of the roof.

Mandie and her friends sat with the adults at a table in the shade and watched and listened. By the way the Italian people greeted one another in such a loud, friendly manner, Mandie felt sure everyone knew everyone else.

"The Italian language sounds so different, doesn't it?" Mandie remarked.

"Yes," Senator Morton agreed. "The language sounds higher pitched, while French is more nasal.

Celia raised her head and sniffed the air. "What is that mouth-watering smell?" she asked.

Mrs. Taft smiled. "You must smell the garlic. The Italians use it in almost everything."

"Garlic?" Mandie asked. "What's that?"

"A cousin to the onion, I suppose," her grandmother explained. "It's strong and often leaves an offensive odor on your breath."

"The Italian rolls are absolutely delicious," Jonathan remarked. "I could eat half a dozen with nothing but butter."

"Italy is also known for their fine cheese," Senator Morton commented. "They usually serve a variety of cheeses with the meal. Of course olives are a standard item on the table, too."

"And don't forget tomatoes," Mrs. Taft reminded him. "Their tomatoes don't look or taste exactly like ours, but they are good." She looked up. "Here's the waiter. Let's make our order so we can make more stops today," she urged.

Since the girls couldn't read Italian and the adults could barely wade through the menu, the senator finally asked the waiter to bring them chicken and vegetables with pasta.

"*Sí, sí, signor.*" The waiter bowed and left with the order. "Where else are we going today?" Mandie asked her grandmother.

"I thought y'all might like to see the Capitol and perhaps the Colosseum," Mrs. Taft suggested.

"Great!" Mandie exclaimed. The others nodded their approval.

Mandie and Celia were so excited that they ate without paying much attention to what it was. They were too hungry to be concerned about the taste, finishing long before the others did. Even Snowball gobbled his food from the saucer under the table.

Jonathan smiled at the girls. "I know you'll like the Capitol," he said. "The huge flight of stairs leading up to it was designed by Michelangelo for Charles the Fifth in 1536. He was the Holy Roman Emperor then. Michelangelo also designed the *Piazza del Campidoglio*, the courtyard in front of the Capitol. And wait till you see the statue of Marcus Aurelius! It's the only bronze equestrian statue that has survived ancient Rome."

"Oh, Jonathan, I wish I had the knowledge you have about so many things," Mandie said. "You seem to know something about everything."

Jonathan laughed. "No, no. I just learned some things in all the private schools I've been to. Besides, I've had the advantage of living in Europe and taking a lot of school tours. Someday you girls will know more about it all, too."

"I hope so," Celia replied.

"Grandmother, do you think the school Celia and I go to will ever go on a tour of Europe?" Mandie asked.

Mrs. Taft smiled. "I doubt that very seriously, dear. I can't envision Miss Hope or Miss Prudence supervising a group of girls through a foreign country, can you?"

Mandie thought for a moment as she fingered the handle on her tea cup. "I guess not."

"But you don't have to worry about that, because I hope we can make more journeys to Europe in the coming years," her grandmother promised. "Longer ones, too."

"We will?" Mandie's blue eyes sparkled. "Oh, thank you, Grandmother!"

"In fact, I've even thought of talking to your mother about sending you to school in England or France for a year or so," Mrs. Taft added, smiling.

Mandie's blue eyes clouded with hesitation. "But, Grandmother, I wouldn't want to be gone from home so long . . . away from all my friends!"

"Perhaps Celia's mother would agree to send her to the same school," Mrs. Taft said, turning to the girl.

Celia smiled faintly. "I don't think I'd want to stay away from my mother for so long."

"Well, it's just an idea for you girls to think about," Mrs. Taft said. "Remember, you are both growing up and can't stay tied to your mothers' apron strings forever. You will need a good education for the future, both of you, considering the inheritance due you someday."

Mandie sighed. With a small quaver in her voice she said, "I know, Grandmother, but I actually count the days at school in Asheville until I can be home again with Mother."

Her grandmother reached across the table to squeeze Mandie's hand. "Dear, let's talk about this when we return home. I didn't mean to upset you." Turning to Senator Morton, Mrs. Taft asked, "Shall we go? I believe everyone is ready."

"To the Capitol!" the senator announced.

Soon the young people were excitedly viewing the Capitol from the carriage that stopped in front of the huge structure. Then alighting, Senator Morton and Mrs. Taft led the way as they slowly climbed the huge flight of stairs Jonathan had told them about.

The adults hurried them through the Capitol, reminding them that if they wanted to see the Colosseum that afternoon, they couldn't spend too much time here. The girls had caught a glimpse of the ancient structure in the distance, and they were eager to see it.

When their carriage finally took them to the Colosseum, the young people couldn't wait to get out.

Mandie and Celia stopped in the middle of the street to stare at the remains of the enormous amphitheater before them.

Mandie gasped. "Oh, it's so big up close!" she exclaimed. "Can we go inside?"

"That's what we plan to do, dear," Mrs. Taft said. She and the senator led the way.

Inside, the girls looked across the vast structure. Senator Morton told them that it was 205 yards in diameter. They walked up and down the old stone steps that were still standing, and sat on the stone wall to look down into the arena.

"The gladiators fought here," the senator said, as he and Mrs. Taft sat down nearby. "In those days it was customary to fight until one of them died. The Emperor Constantine and his successor tried to stop the fights, but the Romans wouldn't give up what to them was their greatest form of entertainment."

"Entertainment? Seeing people killed?" Mandie shivered at the thought as she looked down into the arena of death.

"That was the Romans' way of thinking," Senator Morton replied. "Then at the beginning of the fifth century, a monk from the East named Telemachus walked into the arena and tried to stop the fighting. He begged the people to put a end to these horrible shows, but instead the people stoned the monk to death. However, from that day on the fighting ceased."

The young people silently contemplated what the senator had related.

"He sacrificed himself for the sake of others," Mandie said to herself. "How could those people kill him?"

Mrs. Taft leaned forward. "Back then people didn't live or think like we do now," she said. "The world has become more civilized."

"I hope I live to see the whole world civilized, and living the way God wants us to live," Mandie replied, wiping a tear from her eye.

Senator Morton stood up quickly. "Well, shall we go? We must have some dinner before we go see that magician tonight."

Mandie jumped up. "Is it tonight we are going to see George Rushton perform?"

The senator helped Mrs. Taft to her feet. "Remember, we discussed it last night, and the senator has already bought tickets," she said.

"That's right! Thank you, Senator Morton," Mandie said turning to the silver-haired man.

"Thanks," Celia and Jonathan added.

The senator smiled and turned to lead the way outside. He and Mrs. Taft moved carefully among the precarious stone steps, and the young people trailed behind.

As they descended one level, Mandie stopped to look down into the arena again. She saw a brown flash behind one of the Roman columns below. "Look!" Mandie said, pointing to the arena. "Someone in a deerskin jacket." Her voice was filled with excitement.

"A deerskin jacket?" Jonathan questioned as he and Celia looked to see what Mandie was talking about.

"It must be Uncle Ned!" Mandie exclaimed, hurrying down the steps. "It has to be Uncle Ned!"

Her friends followed her.

"How could it be your Uncle Ned here in Italy, Mandie?" Jonathan asked. "You must be mistaken."

"I didn't see anything," Celia remarked.

"Don't you remember?" Mandie called over her shoulder as she ran toward the arena. "When we saw Uncle Ned in Paris, he told us my mother had sent him over on another ship to look after us while we're in Europe. And he did say he'd see me later."

"But, Mandie," Jonathan argued, trying to keep up

with her, "he said he had business to attend to."

"He only meant he had friends to visit in Europe," Mandie explained. "He has friends everywhere. Everyone knows Uncle Ned, even the President of the United States! Remember, he was invited to the White House too." Mandie continued to lead the way.

The adults had taken a longer, safer route. Mrs. Taft glanced back now and then to see that the young people were following.

"Why does Uncle Ned always hide?" Jonathan asked.

"Because some people are afraid of Indians," Mandie replied, keeping her attention on the exit below. "Besides, he promised my father he would look after me, and I think he stays hidden so he can keep an eye on other people around me."

As Mandie reached the bottom step, a low bird whistle greeted her, and Uncle Ned stepped out from behind a column.

"Uncle Ned!" Mandie exclaimed. She ran to embrace the old man. "I knew it was you. And I knew you'd catch up with us after you'd visited your friends."

The old Indian smiled broadly. "Uncle Ned must be sure Papoose all right," he said, patting the top of Mandie's head.

If only Uncle Ned had been with us in the cata-combs, Mandie thought.

Just then Mrs. Taft and Senator Morton joined them.

"Oh, Uncle Ned!" Mrs. Taft said in surprise. "How nice to see you again."

After greetings were exchanged, Mandie's grand-mother asked, "Will you be staying with us at the hotel?"

"Now and then," Uncle Ned answered.

"Now and then?" Mrs. Taft looked puzzled. "What do you mean by that?"

"Have room in hotel, but also have friends," he explained.

"Oh, you have a room in our hotel!" Mandie repeated excitedly. "Can you go sightseeing with us?"

"Maybe," the old Indian told her.

But the old Indian had other plans for that night. He promised to be in touch again soon. So Senator Morton suggested that they dine in the hotel. He promised to take them to a real Italian restaurant the next night, depending upon how much time they spent sightseeing the next day.

When they returned to their room before dinner, Mandie and Celia discussed their ordeal at the catacombs while they got ready for the evening.

As they relaxed on the big bed in their robes, Celia sighed and said, "Mandie, I dread going back to that place."

Mandie flopped over on her stomach, being careful not to wake Snowball, who was snoozing at the foot of the bed. "I do, too," she said, "but Grandmother wants to go back, and I don't think we should tell her what happened. It'll just upset her, and she might decide to go home . . . or at least leave Italy."

Celia pushed back her long, auburn hair and looked at her friend. "Mandie, do you think that's the honest thing to do?"

"Well, we aren't telling a lie, or anything," Mandie reasoned. "If Grandmother should ask us anything about where we went, I'll tell her the truth. But she and the senator didn't even miss us. We must not have been lost for very long."

"It seemed like ages to me." Celia sighed again.

"I think that is the scariest place I've ever been," Mandie said. "Here we are in the middle of a foreign country where people can't even understand what we say. . . . It's a wonder we got out. The first monk must have told the other one that we were in that room."

"I suppose it shocked the monks, having strange people invade their private domain," Celia remarked.

"Well, I guarantee we'll stick together tomorrow. I won't let Grandmother and the senator out of my sight," Mandie promised.

"Speaking of your grandmother," Celia said, "It must be about time to get dressed, so we won't keep her and the others waiting."

That night Mandie wore a lavender voile dress. The candlelight at the dinner table made her eyes appear deep purple. Celia's batiste dress was cream-colored, which highlighted the golden glints in her auburn hair.

Of course Mrs. Taft and the senator were also dressed elegantly. And Jonathan wore a new suit.

While they were eating, people passing by turned to take a second look at them.

"Do y'all feel like everyone is staring at us?" Mandie whispered.

"Why, yes, dear," Mrs. Taft said. "I suppose they are. Anyone can see we are not Italians. And many people have the idea that all Americans are wealthy." She laughed at the thought.

Mandie smiled. "I thought maybe there was something wrong with my dress," she said.

Snowball meowed from beneath the table, where he was tied to the leg with his red leash.

Mandie looked down at him. "Maybe they noticed

Snowball, too. I suppose it's unusual to have a cat in the hotel dining room."

"Oh, indeed it is," Mrs. Taft agreed. "I had to do some quick talking to accomplish that," she said, leaning toward Mandie.

When they had finished their meal, they took a carriage to the theater where the magician was performing.

As they walked up the theater steps, Jonathan remarked, "Now if you girls will watch very closely, you'll be able to figure out this man's tricks. There's really no such thing as magic, you know."

They followed the adults through the brightly lit doorway of the theater. "Oh, you're just trying to spoil everything for us," she protested. "I don't believe you. I think there is some kind of magic."

"All right, watch and see for yourself," Jonathan told her.

After the Senator presented their tickets, they made their way down the aisle of the theater and were seated near the front. As Mandie sat down between her grandmother and Jonathan, she looked around. The theater was enormous. There were several balconies and a few private alcoves. Overhead, half a dozen electrically lit chandeliers illuminated the huge room. The curtains were closed on the stage, but a band sat ready to play in the pit below.

Mandie leaned over to her grandmother and whispered, "Why don't we have places like this back home?"

"We do, dear. You have never been to the big cities," Mrs. Taft explained in a loud whisper. The band began playing and Mrs. Taft spoke up. "I'll have to take you to New York some time. Of course, it's not as old as the cities in Europe, but it's very large."

A sudden loud blast from the band drowned out their conversation. The curtain opened, and everyone leaned forward to watch. To their amazement, the stage was completely empty.

The music softened to a waltz tune, and various props "floated" onto the stage, propelled by an unseen force. An organ grinder's cart—without the organ grinder— came rolling in from the left and stopped at center stage. Then a small jewelry box slid along the floor and came to rest beside the cart. From the right an enormous silver cage containing a live monkey rolled in and bumped into the cart.

Mandie turned to Jonathan and whispered, "What makes everything move? There's no one up there."

The music grew louder and picked up tempo. Jonathan tried to explain, but the music didn't allow him to be heard. He leaned close to Mandie's ear and yelled, "I'll tell you later."

Mandie quickly put her hand over her ear and moved away from Jonathan as she continued to watch the stage.

Suddenly, from the ceiling above the stage George Rushton, dressed in a black tuxedo with a black silk top hat, descended in a golden cage suspended on ropes clearly visible to the audience. When the cage reached the floor, he quickly stepped out and waved a white handkerchief, greeting the crowd.

As he passed the handkerchief through his hand, it turned into several handkerchiefs of various colors. The people applauded enthusiastically.

The magician bowed, took off his top hat and pulled a white rabbit out of it. The audience again applauded.

Mandie grabbed her grandmother's arm in excitement. She had never seen anything like this.

Then George Rushton placed the rabbit in the silver cage and led the monkey out by a ribbon. The monkey jumped on top of the organ grinder's cart and danced as the band played. He was dressed in a tiny tuxedo, and when the music stopped, he stopped dancing, took off his top hat and bowed to the wild applause of the audience. Then the monkey jumped down and returned to the silver cage, which also held the rabbit.

As the music softened again, the magician finally spoke to the crowd. Picking up the jewelry case on the floor, he said, "Ladies and gentlemen, I show you an empty case."

He opened the box and shook it for the audience to see. "I will now close the empty box," he said. "From this handkerchief I will make a stone fit for a king appear inside the empty box." He pulled another white handkerchief out of his pocket with one hand while he held the box in the other.

Shaking out the handkerchief, the magician draped it over the box. "Now when I remove this handkerchief, please watch closely." He slowly turned toward the audience. His gaze swept from one side to the other. Keeping the box covered, he called out, "Are you ready?"

"Yes!" the crowd shouted back in unison.

Slowly, he slid the handkerchief off the empty box. Then, opening the lid, he held out the contents for everyone to see. What looked like a giant-sized ruby lay on the black velvet lining.

The audience oohed and aahed in wonder. Then as they watched, George Rushton reversed his act and made the stone disappear again.

"Well!" Mandie exclaimed. "I wonder how he did that!"

"Easy," Jonathan replied.

Without turning her gaze from the stage Mandie whispered, "I'd like to see you do that since you know so much about it."

"I could if I had his equipment," Jonathan told her.

The volume of the music increased and George Rushton performed several other acts. Mandie and Jonathan didn't have another opportunity to talk.

However, in the carriage on the way back to the hotel the young people discussed every detail of the show.

Mandie said to Jonathan, "So, you think you could do what he did if you had his equipment."

Jonathan smiled mischievously. "Sure, nothing to it."

"He's staying in our hotel. Let's see if he brings his equipment with him. And if he does, maybe he'll let you use it to show me how it's done," Mandie suggested.

"Oh, he'd never agree to that," Jonathan said. "That would give away his secrets."

"Of course it would," Celia agreed.

The carriage came to a halt at the front door of their hotel.

Mandie smiled at Jonathan. "We'll see."

"Tonight?" Celia asked as they rose to leave the carriage.

"No, it's too late tonight, but as soon as I get a chance I'll ask him," Mandie promised.

Chapter 6 / Trouble in the Catacombs

The next morning was bright and sunny, and after an early breakfast, Mandie and her friends went with her grandmother and Senator Morton back to the catacombs.

The young people whispered to each other during the carriage ride there while the adults carried on their own conversation.

"I wonder if we could find those monks again," Mandie said softly.

"Oh, no, Mandie!" Celia objected. "Let's not go looking for them."

"I really don't think we ought to try to find them," Jonathan agreed. "We might get lost again, and Mrs. Taft and Senator Morton wouldn't like it at all."

Mandie smoothed Snowball's white fur. "It just bothers me that so many mysterious things seem to happen to us, as if people are trying to hurt us or get us distracted."

"But, Mandie, we don't know that anyone at the catacombs was trying to do something to us," Celia reminded her.

"That's right," Jonathan said. "I think we just got lost and went into a section where visitors are not allowed."

"I'm not so sure about that," Mandie replied. "After all, I did see that strange woman there."

"That's true," Jonathan said with a sigh. "But I'll tell you right now, if you go wandering off looking for those monks, I will not go with you."

Mandie looked at Celia who was silent and avoiding Mandie's gaze.

Mandie shrugged her shoulders. "Oh, well, who can tell what might happen this time?"

Their carriage pulled up in front of the catacombs amid a group of uniformed school children, whose teachers were herding them into lines headed toward the entrance.

Mrs. Taft stepped down from the vehicle. "Hurry, dears," she called to Mandie and her friends. "Let's see if we can get ahead of all these children."

The young people quickly followed the adults inside. Mrs. Taft stopped to speak to them. "The senator and I never did get into the recesses below yesterday, and that's what we'd like to do today," she explained. "Be sure you stay within sight of us at all times."

"Yes, ma'am," the three answered together.

They looked at one another and smiled as they followed Mrs. Taft and Senator Morton down the stone stairs into the caverns below.

"Why don't we go to the left here and see if it circles back," Mrs. Taft said, leading the way into a large room lighted by candles.

"I don't believe we were in here yesterday," Mandie

said as she tried to read a plaque on the wall. "What does this say, Jonathan? Can you decipher it?"

Jonathan moved closer. "It's Latin," he said. "I have to take it in school next year, but right now I couldn't tell you what it says."

Down the length of the room they found other plaques in Latin with Italian translations alongside them. Mandie felt frustrated that none of the three could read the inscriptions.

They wandered to the far end, and found an alcove with only a half wall dividing it from the rest of the room. The floor was covered with tiny loose stones, and Mandie suddenly felt something in her shoe.

"Wait!" she cried, stopping at the half wall. "I have to check my shoe. Something's stuck in it." She handed Snowball to Celia and placed her bag on top of the partition.

The chatter of dozens of school children came closer until the room was filled with them. They spoke rapidly in Italian, and the teachers had all they could do to control them.

Mandie unbuttoned her shoe and a tiny pebble fell out from between the buttons. Jonathan offered a hand to steady her as she put her shoe back on. Then she stooped to fasten it.

The schoolchildren left as suddenly as they had entered.

Mandie breathed a sigh of relief. "I'm glad they decided to move on," she said, straightening her long skirt and adjusting her bonnet. "There are so many of them, and they are so noisy."

"Yes, our teachers never let us talk that loudly in a

group," Celia agreed. "At least not at that age."

Mandie reached for her purse on the half wall and gasped. "My bag! Where did it go?" she exclaimed, quickly scanning the floor around the partition. "I put it right here."

"I know. I saw it there," Celia confirmed. She handed Snowball back to Mandie, and she and Jonathan began searching the alcove.

"Maybe one of those children picked it up," Jonathan suggested.

"Let's catch up to them and find out," Mandie quickly replied.

The three hurried down the length of the room to where Mrs. Taft and the senator were reading plaques.

"I lost my bag, Grandmother," Mandie explained hastily. "One of those children might have picked it up. We're going to see."

"Then we'll go with you," Mrs. Taft said. "I don't see how you could have lost it."

As they hurried back to the entrance, Mandie explained what had happened.

"I'm sorry, dear," Mrs. Taft said. "Perhaps one of those youngsters did pick it up by mistake."

They got all the way to the front door just in time to see the carriages full of children leave.

"They're gone!" Mandie exclaimed. "And we don't even know who they were."

"I suppose that's the last of that," Mrs. Taft remarked. "Amanda, you should be more careful of your belongings. You'll probably never see that bag again."

"I'm sorry, Grandmother," Mandie said, frowning. "I guess I was careless."

"Are you sure one of those children took it?" Senator Morton asked. "Maybe it fell behind something. Let's go take another look."

"Yes, we should," Mrs. Taft agreed, turning to lead the way back inside.

By using hand motions and a mix of French and English, Senator Morton was able to enlist the help of the guard at the entrance. The tall, young Italian smiled sympathetically at Mandie and searched all along the way as they walked back to the alcove where the bag had disappeared.

The guard and the young people stooped to examine the floor, but the bag was nowhere to be found.

The young man finally stood and looked at Mandie in dismay. "No bag, Signorina," he said.

Mandie couldn't hide her disappointment. "Thank you for looking," she said sadly.

"*Grazie*," Senator Morton told the young man. "Thank you very much."

"*Prego*," the guard replied. "You are welcome." He bowed slightly and went back to his station at the entrance of the catacombs.

Mrs. Taft looked at her granddaughter. "I'll buy you another bag, Mandie."

"Thank you, Grandmother, but I did bring another bag with me to Europe," Mandie replied weakly. "That one just happened to be my favorite. I took it everywhere."

"What did you carry in it, dear?" her grandmother asked.

"I don't really know," Mandie said. "I've been trying to remember. Let me see—I think I had a handkerchief, a comb, and a little money in it."

"Is that all?" Senator Morton asked.

"I think so," Mandie replied.

"Then there was nothing that can't be replaced," Mrs. Taft said. "Now let's get on with our tour."

As the group slowly made their way through the catacombs, Mandie and her friends watched carefully for any signs of her bag. They scrutinized everyone they passed, looking to see what each person was carrying. They also searched the stone floors as they followed Mrs. Taft and the senator through the maze of tombs. But there was no sign of Mandie's bag.

Mrs. Taft and Senator Morton entered a small room at the end of a long corridor, and Mandie heard her grandmother greet someone. The young people pushed forward to see who it was.

"Good morning," Mrs. Taft said courteously. "Imagine seeing you here."

"Good morning, Mrs. Taft," a male voice replied. "I am delighted to see you and the senator again."

Mandie gasped and said, "It's Mr. Rushton."

The man kept looking from one side to the other, as if in a hurry to go on. "If you will excuse me, I hope to see you all later." He quickly proceeded down the passageway.

Mandie watched him go, and when he got to the end of the corridor, he stopped to speak to another man. The candlelight was too dim to make out what the other man looked like. The two disappeared around the bend.

Mandie turned to Jonathan. "I wish I could have spoken to him. I would have asked him if you could use his equipment to show us some magic, Jonathan."

"Mandie, you know that man isn't going to let anyone touch his equipment," Jonathan insisted.

"You never know till you ask," Mandie replied.

Mandie and her friends caught up with her grandmother and the senator, but they quickly became bored with the place. Time seemed to drag. There were so many other things to see in Rome. Mandie wanted to move on.

The young people were relieved when the adults finally decided to leave.

"I believe we have seen about all there is to see, dears," Mrs. Taft said. "Everything else is just more of the same. Shall we go now?"

"Yes, ma'am," the three quickly answered.

"I don't know about you young folks, but something tells me it's time to have some more of that good Italian food," Senator Morton said with a smile.

"Yes, sir," the young people agreed.

They walked quickly through the passageways, and on upstairs. As they arrived at the top step, they were shocked to see policemen everywhere.

"My goodness!" Mandie cried. "What's happened now?"

A policeman standing near the stairs stepped forward to speak to the senator. He was carrying a small notebook.

"Please, Signor, may I have your names and where you are from and where you are staying?" the policeman asked in perfect British English. He looked from one to the other of the group.

Senator Morton pulled their papers out of his pocket

and handed them to the policeman. "Of course," he said. "I believe you will find the information you need for all of us right here."

The man took the papers and began copying information from them into his notebook.

"What has happened, officer?" Mrs. Taft asked.

"There has been a robbery, Signora," the man said without looking up. "We must take all names and addresses of visitors and investigate."

"You're not talking about my bag, are you?" Mandie quickly asked.

The man stopped writing and smiled at her. "Signorina, I do not know anything about your bag. What is missing is the very large ruby from that case over there." He pointed across the room toward the display case the young people had looked into the day before. He bent over his notebook again.

Mandie said, "My bag was stolen, too. At least I think it was stolen. Anyway it just disappeared."

The policeman looked up again. "If you will please stop by our headquarters and make up a report, we will be happy to pursue the matter for you," he said patiently. "Right now we must expend every effort to find the ruby. It is part of our national heritage."

"Thank you. I understand," Mandie replied. "And I'm sorry about your ruby. I sincerely hope you find it."

The policeman finished taking the information and returned the papers to Senator Morton. "Thank you. You may proceed now," he said.

Mrs. Taft walked slowly past the case where the ruby had been. "My, my, what a loss!" she exclaimed. "I remember seeing the stone."

As they went outside, Senator Morton said, "They have a good police force here in Rome. They'll probably find it. Whoever took it must still be in the catacombs."

The young people lagged behind.

"And the catacombs have more levels than most people realize," Mandie whispered to her friends.

"Yes, it's a perfect place for thieves to hide," Jonathan said quietly.

"They would have to know this place pretty well, or they'd get lost and maybe never find their way out," Celia added.

"You are so right," Mandie agreed. "But you know, I just don't understand how anyone could have stolen the ruby. It was locked in that case, and there's also a guard there. Remember, he came and looked for my bag for me."

"That's right," Jonathan said. "Whoever took the ruby must be a professional thief. No one saw him."

"Him or *her*," Mandie added.

"Oh, Mandie, do you really think that strange woman could have been involved in this?" Celia asked nervously.

Mandie's heart sank. "I don't know," she said. "But I feel so awful about asking the guard to help me find my bag. Maybe that's when the thief took the ruby!"

Jonathan tried to console her. "You had no way of knowing. . . . Besides, whoever took it would have found a way, with or without the guard gone looking for your bag."

"We should tell someone," Celia urged.

"What would we tell them?" Jonathan asked. "We can't prove any of this."

Mrs. Taft stopped in front of a bench in the middle of a flower garden and sat down. "Let's sit here while Senator Morton finds a carriage for us," she suggested. The young people sat down with her. Senator Morton hurried down the road.

Mandie allowed Snowball to roam on his leash, and he immediately began to scamper in the grass.

"Whew! I didn't realize I was tired until I sat down," Mrs. Taft said, fanning herself with her white lace handkerchief. "It's so warm out here after being in that cold place. But it was awfully interesting, didn't y'all think so?"

"Yes, ma'am," Mandie agreed. The others nodded.

"I don't believe we would ever be able to cover the entire place," Mrs. Taft continued. "There are so many nooks and crannies and passageways and steps. The Franciscan monks are the custodians of the place, but I certainly didn't see a single one."

The young people exchanged glances.

"They probably have private living quarters where the public can't go," Mrs. Taft rambled on.

Jonathan cleared his throat.

Mandie, believing he was about to speak, quickly said, "They wouldn't allow visitors to invade their private rooms, I'm sure."

"No," Jonathan agreed. "It might scare the monks, for one thing. I don't imagine they are used to mixing with other people."

"I, for one, wouldn't want to go visiting monks," Celia added.

Mrs. Taft rose. "I see Senator Morton waving at us," she said. "Let's go." She started for the carriage the senator had procured.

Mandie picked up Snowball, and the young people lagged behind again so they could talk quietly.

Mandie nudged Jonathan. "I thought for a minute you were going to tell my grandmother that we had seen some of the monks," she whispered.

"Do I look that dumb?" Jonathan replied sharply.

"Of course not," Mandie answered, "but sometimes a person says things without thinking."

"Speak for yourself," Jonathan teased.

"Sorry," Mandie whispered.

They all boarded the carriage, and Senator Morton took them to an inside restaurant for the midday meal. The decor was done entirely in black and white—the tile, the murals on the walls, the furniture, the china, even the tablecloths were of a black-and-white-checked fabric.

The waiter didn't speak a word of English and couldn't understand anything they were saying. He had to get another man, apparently the owner, to take their order. But he didn't know much English, either. Finally, Senator Morton gave up and simply said, "*Ravioli*."

The man smiled broadly. "Ah, *ravioli!*" he said, and rushed off to get their food.

"What is *ravioli*?" Mandie asked.

The senator tried to explain: "It's like macaroni, only shaped in squares and filled with meat or cheese. It is served in a spicy tomato sauce," he said. "I think you will all like it. If you don't, we'll try something else."

When the food came, however, the young people ate eagerly, finding the dish very tasty. Even Snowball seemed to enjoy the portion that Mandie put on a saucer under the table.

After a while, the conversation turned to the theft at the catacombs.

Mrs. Taft showed her concern. "I feel sorry for these people," she said. "Imagine how it would feel to have a national treasure stolen in our United States!"

Mandie dropped her fork suddenly onto her plate. "I just had a great idea! I wonder if the Italians are offering a reward for the return of the ruby. Maybe we could find it and collect the reward!"

"Amanda!" Mrs. Taft said sharply. "Don't even consider such an idea. We will not become involved in this. It doesn't concern us."

Mandie meekly dropped her gaze. "Yes, Grandmother," she said. "We won't get into what is not our business." Then under her breath, she added, "But I sure wish we could."

Jonathan and Celia glanced at her in alarm.

Chapter 7 / Out of the Past

That afternoon they continued their sightseeing, and it was a day never to be forgotten by Mandie. The Bible came alive for her.

The senator took them to see St. Paul Outside the Walls, the most illustrious church in Rome and the burial place of the apostle Paul. As they alighted from their carriage, Senator Morton told them the story.

In awe, Mandie and her friends walked toward the giant stone structure.

"You mean the Paul in the Bible? He's buried here?" Mandie could hardly believe it.

"That's what the Italians say," Mrs. Taft replied.

Mandie and Celia held hands as they gazed about them. The portico was composed of 150 columns, and a statue of the apostle Paul stood in the center. Mosaics on the facade glittered with gold and many other colors.

Inside, the senator directed them to a marble casket. "This sarcophagus is claimed to contain the remains of the apostle Paul," he said.

Mandie felt her knees weaken as she stared. "I know

the Bible is true," she said, "but this makes it all so real to me."

"And to me," Celia whispered, squeezing Mandie's hand.

Jonathan kicked at nothing on the floor and turned around.

When they had seen everything they wanted to see at St. Paul's, the senator took them to St. Pietro in Vincoli, which in English means St. Peter in Chains. Here they viewed the chains used by Herod to keep Peter in prison.

And then they saw the famous statue of Moses by Michelangelo. As Mandie stared up at the immense sculpture, she felt as though Moses would come alive any moment. He looked so real, so majestic.

Mandie and Celia held hands most of the afternoon for support as they viewed the realities of the past. Jonathan volunteered to carry Snowball, who was well behaved for a change.

By the time they finally returned to their hotel late that afternoon, Mandie and Celia collapsed with fatigue on their big bed. Mrs. Taft had told them to get some rest before dinner, and they gratefully complied.

"Oh, Celia, I wish I could have lived when Jesus was living on earth," Mandie told her friend. She turned over on her stomach and propped up on her elbows. "The people who actually knew Jesus then were the luckiest people who ever lived on this earth."

"I agree, Mandie, but it would have been terrible to live through the time of His crucifixion," Celia reminded her.

"Oh, you're right," Mandie said. "You know, I think this day will be the most important day in all our journey through Europe. Nothing else could compare with it."

"Yes," Celia agreed. "Including the robbery at the catacombs and the disappearance of your purse."

"I still can't remember for sure what I had in my bag," Mandie said pensively. "I suppose it was nothing important. Anyway, whatever it was, it's gone now."

"Too bad," Celia murmured.

Suddenly Mandie bounced off the bed. "Come to think of it, I have to find my other bag to take tonight." She went to the bureau and began opening drawers until she found it.

"Here it is," she said, holding up an embroidered drawstring bag of various colors. "With all these colors, it goes with everything I have. Now I have to find an extra comb and a handkerchief." Finding these in another drawer, she put them in the bag.

Celia sat up on the side of the bed. "You had some money in your other bag, too, didn't you?" she asked.

"Yes, but Grandmother still has some of my money, if I need it," Mandie said, pulling the strings on the bag shut.

Celia got up and fetched her bag from a nearby chair. She opened it and pulled out a roll of paper money. "Here, Mandie, I'd like to share what I have with you. Take this." She held out about half the bills to her friend.

"No, Celia," Mandie protested. "My grandmother has more of my money. I can't take yours."

"Mandie, this is an opportunity for me to share something with you," Celia insisted. "You're my best friend, and you're always so patient and considerate. I'd just like to give you something."

Mandie sighed. "Well, if you insist. I'll buy something nice to remind me of Rome and say that you gave it to me. Will that be all right?" She took the proffered bills and stuffed them into her bag.

Celia smiled. "Whatever you want to do with it is all right with me," she agreed.

At that moment Mrs. Taft knocked and then opened the door. "Girls, it's time to get dressed for dinner," she said. "And please wear something special. Senator Morton is taking us to the *Roma Ristorante*, which is probably the most expensive place in Rome. You have about thirty minutes. And, Amanda, this is one time you'll have to leave Snowball here. Just lock him in the bathroom. He'll be all right."

"Yes, Grandmother," Mandie said.

Mrs. Taft left the room and closed the door.

The girls hurriedly flipped through their clothes in the huge wardrobe. Mandie chose her blue silk dress and Celia her yellow silk. They were dressed and waiting by the time Mrs. Taft returned. Mandie put a pillow in the bathtub and set Snowball on it, admonishing him to behave while she was gone. Then she locked the bathroom door.

Senator Morton was able to get a public carriage right away, and they were soon on their way. They traveled through a part of the city where the young people had not been before. They enjoyed the ride and the scenery. Soon the driver pulled up in front of a huge marble building with bright electric lights illuminating the whole area.

An attendant assisted everyone from the carriage, and the girls looked around with excitement.

Mandie's blue eyes sparkled. "All these electric lights are going to have us spoiled," she said. "Everything is so much brighter than with oil or gas lamps."

"You probably don't know it, but the people of Franklin are getting up a petition to have electricity run into your town," her grandmother replied. "And if they do, your mother will get it, I'm sure."

"It might be all right in our house," Mandie said, glancing at the many light bulbs overhead as they entered the restaurant. "We're supposed to get it at our school sometime, too."

"Yes, lots of places in Asheville already have it," Mrs. Taft told her. She turned to take the senator's arm to enter the dining room.

Jonathan stepped between the girls and held out both arms. "My pleasure, young ladies," he said with his mischievous smile.

Mandie and Celia each took an arm, and they followed the adults into the dining room. Mandie's dress was a little too long, and she had to be careful not to trip on it.

The head waiter led them all to a table near a small platform where a trio of uniformed men were tuning their musical instruments.

After everyone was seated, Mandie looked about the room. Almost every table was occupied. All the diners looked well dressed, and were of many different nationalities.

All at once, for no reason at all, Mandie felt terribly homesick—homesick for her mother and her stepfather, who was also her Uncle John, and for her lifetime friend, Joe Woodard. Joe—what would he think of this place and the countries they had been to? And the mysterious events that had happened? A slight smile curved her lips as she stared into space. Joe was always trying to keep her out of trouble, but he usually managed to become involved before her adventures ended.

Celia nudged her friend. "Mandie!" she whispered.

Mandie came back to the present with a start. Her grandmother was waiting to hear what Mandie wanted to order.

"I'm sorry, Grandmother. My mind was back in North Carolina," Mandie said.

Mrs. Taft looked at her with concern. "I hope you don't get homesick, dear," she said. "We have lots more traveling to do. But right now we must order our food."

The waiter, who stood patiently beside Senator Morton, smiled at Mandie.

"What do they have, Grandmother?" Mandie asked.

"Dear, the waiter just ran down a long list, but we've all decided to have ham," Mrs. Taft explained. "It's familiar to us, and it's rather late for us to be eating a big meal. But they also have many kinds of vegetables and salads." She looked up at the waiter, who immediately ran through his list again for Mandie.

Mandie shrugged. "I guess I'll have ham, too," she said. "And I'll have to take Snowball something to eat."

"No, dear, that would be too messy," Mrs. Taft told her. "We can get something at our hotel for him, I'm sure."

Before long, they were all enjoying their meal. The musicians roamed the dining room as they played and sang Italian songs, and they gave special attention to Mandie and her friends. They stopped at the end of the table and played several soft tunes. Mandie, Celia, and Jonathan eagerly applauded. Senator Morton dropped money into the cloth bag which hung from the shoulder of one of the men.

Then as the senator and Mrs. Taft held their own conversation at the other end of the table, the young people spoke quietly among themselves.

Mandie said to her friends, "This is more fun than the dining room in our hotel. I wish we could come here every night."

"It would be awfully expensive, I imagine," Celia replied.

"I don't think we'll be spending much more time here in Italy, anyway," Jonathan told the girls. "In order to visit all the places your grandmother has planned for you to see, I'd think we'd be going on into Switzerland soon."

Mandie looked at him. "I hadn't thought about that," she said. "Yes, we do have a limited amount of time, so we have to spread it over several countries. Maybe we can come back to Europe next summer."

Jonathan looked worried. "I have no idea what my father will do about me." He sighed. "I'd rather go home to New York and go to school there. I've been to so many foreign schools."

"It would be nice if you could stay home with your father and go to school there," Mandie said with a wistful smile. "That's what I wanted to do. I tried to get my mother to let me stay home and go to school in Franklin, but she thought I'd get a better education at the school Celia and I go to in Asheville."

"But as your grandmother said, Mandie, we can't stay home with our mothers forever," Celia said.

"We could," Mandie quickly replied. "We might have to grow up, but we don't have to get married and leave home."

"Oh, Mandie," Jonathan teased, "you'll get married someday."

Before Mandie could answer, Celia spoke up. "Mandie, you know Joe expects you to marry him when you both grow up. He—"

"Celia!" Mandie quickly interrupted. Her face turned red. "I don't have to marry Joe or anyone else if I don't want to. I wish you'd—"

"I'm sorry, Mandie," Celia said. "I didn't mean to—"

"Girls!" Mrs. Taft spoke sharply. "What is going on? I expect you both to act like young ladies."

"I'm sorry, Grandmother," Mandie said meekly. She glanced at her friend and added, "Please forgive me, Celia. I didn't mean to shout at you."

"That's all right, Mandie," Celia said, smiling. "I started it. I'm sorry, too."

Jonathan smiled mischievously. "Now that we're all sorry, let's change the subject," he said. "Have you girls discussed the robbery at the catacombs today?"

"Well, yes, we did," Mandie told him, "—and the loss of my bag. But we haven't figured out anything new, have you?"

"The senator told me there have been several gem robberies in other countries recently, and it's always a national treasure of some kind," Jonathan said. "The police think these are all connected."

"They do?" Mandie gasped. "You mean there are what you'd call international thieves?"

"Yes, there always have been," Jonathan replied. "These people steal something and then cross over the border into another country so the police can't so easily find them. They probably assume the police can't do anything to them once they're in another county," he explained.

"But they can, can't they?" Celia asked.

"They certainly can," the boy agreed. "The European countries cooperate with each other when it comes to crooks like that."

"I wonder if they'll ever find your bag, Mandie," Celia said.

Mandie shook her head. "No, that's gone," she said. "Grandmother and Senator Morton decided it wasn't worth the trouble to go through a formal police report, so no one is even looking for it."

"That's too bad," Jonathan said sympathetically.

Mandie took a sip of tea. "It doesn't really matter. I don't think I had anything in it that can't be replaced, and I have this other bag." She held up the one she was carrying.

Mrs. Taft caught their attention. "Girls, Jonathan. Senator Morton and I have decided that we'll travel on into Switzerland this weekend. So y'all need to let us know if there is anything else you especially want to see here in Rome in the next two days."

The young people looked at each other and thought for a moment.

Jonathan spoke first. "You girls may want to see Trevi Fountain," he said, winking at Mandie. "They say if you throw a coin over your shoulder into the water there, you will return to Rome some day."

"Really!" the girls exclaimed.

"Then let's do go see it." Mandie smiled eagerly at her grandmother.

"Please," Celia added.

"We'll do that tomorrow," Mrs. Taft agreed. "Then there are a couple of other places the senator and I want to visit."

"I'd also like to go back by the entrance to the catacombs, to see if they found the thief who took the ruby," Mandie suggested.

"We won't have to do that," Senator Morton said. "It'll

certainly be in the newspaper when the thief is appre-
hended. And if nothing does appear in the paper before
we leave, we can ask the police."

"Thank you, Senator," Mandie said. "I hadn't even
thought about the newspaper."

Mrs. Taft looked around the table. "If everyone is finished, I think it would be nice to take a stroll before going
back to the hotel," she said.

They all agreed and once they were outside the restaurant, Senator Morton led them through several narrow
cobblestone streets where the local people were walking
about or sitting in small groups conversing animatedly in
their native tongue.

As they passed bakeries and shops of all kinds, Mandie took in deep breaths of air. "Italy even smells different
from France," she said with a laugh. "There's a delicious
edible aroma here."

"It's the highly seasoned foods and wonderful
breads," Mrs. Taft explained.

"The city is noisier, too, I think," Celia added.

Senator Morton laughed. "That's because the Italians
are such fun-loving, friendly people, and they love nothing
better than to talk," he told them.

"I think the French are more dignified," Jonathan
said.

"Well, so far, I love them all in every country," Mandie
decided.

After a long stroll, Senator Morton hired a public carriage and they rode back to their hotel. The day had been
an exciting one.

When they arrived at their hotel, Mrs. Taft told the girls
to get to bed immediately since it had been such a long
day.

There were no arguments.

As Mandie and Celia entered their bedroom, Mandie glanced at the closed bathroom door. "Snowball!" she exclaimed, rushing into the bathroom to get him.

Mandie and Celia found the white kitten curled up in the huge lavatory, sound asleep.

"Look at that," Mandie said. "I make him a nice soft bed in the bathtub, and he climbs up here in the sink." She picked him up.

"Mandie, do you know what we forgot?" Celia asked.

"Food for Snowball!" Mandie exclaimed. "I'll ask Grandmother if I can go downstairs and get something for him."

Mrs. Taft reluctantly agreed, but told the girls to hurry back.

When Mandie and Celia approached the front desk, they were surprised to see George Rushton standing there, talking to the clerk.

"Hello, Mr. Rushton," Mandie greeted him. "Are you already finished with your performance for tonight?"

The magician turned and smiled at the girls. "I didn't have one scheduled for tonight," he said. "However, I am working on setting up a performance right here in the hotel in the next few days. I don't know the exact date. I'll have to let you know, but I would be proud to have you young ladies come."

Mandie and Celia became flustered with the important man's invitation. "Thank you," they managed.

"We have to see what my grandmother has planned before we can say whether or not we can come," Mandie told him.

The clerk spoke up then. "Miss Shaw, I believe we have something here that belongs to you." He stooped under the counter, and when he stood up he held Mandie's missing bag in his hand.

"My bag!" Mandie reached for it. "Where did you get it?"

"Someone left it here on the counter tonight," the clerk explained. "No one saw who it was, but they also left this piece of paper." He handed her a note.

Mandie read it aloud: "Property of Miss Amanda Shaw." She turned the note over. "That's all there is on the paper."

George Rushton looked over Mandie's shoulder at the note. "It would be impossible to identify anyone from that," he said. "But at least you got your bag back."

Mandie examined the purse. It was dirty and looked almost as if it had been dropped in the mud. "It's so soiled I don't know if I will ever use it again," she said, untying the drawstrings. "But it looks like everything is still in it— my money, my comb, and my handkerchief."

Celia examined the stained bag. "Maybe you ought to just throw it away, Mandie," she suggested.

"I think so," Mandie agreed. "I'll just wrap everything in the handkerchief." She spread it out on the counter and rolled the money and comb in it. Turning to the clerk, she said, "Could you please just drop the bag in a waste can?"

"Wait!" George Rushton spoke up. "My maid could wash it for you. She comes in every day, and I could ask her to try to clean it so that you could use it again."

"Oh, would you?" Mandie said, smiling. "That would be so nice of you, Mr. Rushton."

The magician picked up the bag. "No trouble at all," he said. "I should get to my room. I'll leave the bag here at the desk for you."

"Thank you," Mandie called after the tall man as he walked on down the corridor.

"Mandie, what did you do with the note?" Celia asked, looking around.

"Oh, I guess Mr. Rushton took it with the bag. It doesn't matter," Mandie said, turning to the clerk. "I need some food for my kitten. Can you tell me where I could get it?"

"*Sí, sí, Signorina*," the clerk replied with a big smile. "I will have something sent up to your room right away."

Mandie looked at him in surprise. "I don't want to cause extra work for anyone. I could carry it upstairs."

"No, no, I must find a maid," the man explained. "We will send something up soon."

The girls thanked the clerk and returned to their suite. When they got there, Mrs. Taft was relaxing in her robe, reading a book. Mandie told her grandmother about the missing bag turning up at the counter downstairs, and Mr. Rushton's offer to clean it.

"That's strange, dear. You didn't have your name on the bag, did you?" Mrs. Taft asked.

"No, I didn't, Grandmother," Mandie replied. "I don't know how anyone would know the bag belonged to me."

"And your belongings were still in it?" Mrs. Taft asked.

"Yes," Mandie said. "Even the money."

Mrs. Taft looked puzzled.

"If Mr. Rushton's maid can't get it clean," Mandie sighed, "I'll just throw it away. And I might as well forget about the mystery surrounding it."

"That's right, dear," Mrs. Taft said.

Just then a maid came with food for Snowball.

"Feed your kitten, Mandie," Mrs. Taft said, "and then you girls get into bed immediately."

The girls did get right into bed, but they lay awake a long time, discussing the return of Mandie's bag.

"Maybe someone tried to play a joke on you by taking the bag and then bringing it right back," Celia suggested.

"Well, if that's true, it sounds like a crazy joke to me," Mandie said. "Maybe Jonathan will have some ideas tomorrow."

Chapter 8 / Another Mystery

Mandie and Celia were still asleep the next morning when the maid came in and opened the draperies. The bright sunlight woke them. They quickly sat up in bed. Snowball stretched, yawned, and jumped down to the floor.

The maid stood beside their bed in her uniform with a starched white apron and cap. She pointed to the tray on the table nearby and smiled. "Breakfast I have brought," she told them.

"Oh, thank you," both girls replied. They jumped out of bed and went to see what was on the tray.

"Two trays," the woman explained. "One for the lady." She pointed toward the parlor. "And one for the *signorinas*."

She walked toward the door, told the girls goodbye and left.

"I'm starving for some reason," Mandie declared. She pulled up a chair and after returning thanks, she began eating a roll.

Celia poured coffee into the two cups provided and joined her. "I'll get fat from all this traveling," she said, buttering a roll from the covered dish. "It makes me so hungry."

Snowball came to beg. Mandie put a saucer on the floor with a piece of a roll that had bits of ham baked into it.

"I need to catch up on my journal," Mandie told Celia. "You know, I haven't written in it for days."

"It didn't do any good to buy the bags to carry them in because we don't take them with us," Celia said, sipping the strong, hot coffee.

"It's just too much trouble to carry a book around all the time," Mandie decided. "We'll have to remember to write in them when we get the chance. Maybe we could do it now, before Grandmother asks us to get dressed."

"Good idea," Celia said.

The girls quickly finished their food and sat on the bed with their journals opened in their laps.

Mandie thought for a moment and then began hastily writing in her book. Celia did likewise. And by the time Mrs. Taft came to tell them to get ready, both girls had managed to enter the events for each day up to the present.

Mandie closed her journal and placed it back in the mesh bag. She hurried over to her small trunk in the corner, raised the lid and put the book inside, then pushed the lock shut.

Celia frowned. "Mandie, why are you locking up your journal?"

Mandie smiled as she took a dress from the wardrobe. "Well, because I wrote some of my innermost thoughts in that book, and I don't want anybody else reading it."

"I never thought of that. I guess I'd better lock mine up, too." Celia walked over to her own trunk and locked her journal inside. "However, I don't know who would want to read our journals."

Celia started to select a dress for the day, and suddenly turned to Mandie and asked, "Mandie, where are the keys to our trunks? I don't have them."

"Neither do I," Mandie said matter-of-factly. "Grandmother has all the keys to everything, remember?"

"I hope she has these," Celia replied.

The girls dressed hurriedly, and Mandie put the red harness on Snowball and attached the leash. He fought it as usual and rolled over and over trying to get it off.

Mandie tried to straighten out the leash. "Snowball, either you wear the harness or you stay here," she told him. "I'll lock you up in the bathroom again."

Snowball immediately flipped over onto his feet and meowed loudly as he looked up at his mistress.

"Now that's better," Mandie said. She stood up with the end of the leash in her hand.

The white kitten began purring and rubbing around her ankles. The girls went into the parlor and sat down.

"You know, Mandie, he's a smart kitten," Celia remarked. "I think he knows what you're saying."

"He probably knows the different tones of my voice, whether I'm scolding or playing," Mandie said. She sat down again and Celia joined her. "He ought to by this time. You know I brought him from Charley Gap right after I lost my father. He was just a tiny kitten."

Mrs. Taft opened her bedroom door and walked across the parlor to the girls. "Amanda, would you please see if you can get the hook fastened on this necklace?" she asked. "And Celia, please knock on the senator's door and tell him we're ready."

Celia went across the hall. Mrs. Taft turned and sat

on the settee so Mandie could reach the hook.

"Grandmother, isn't this the same necklace you wore to Mr. Rushton's tea, the one I had to unfasten for you before?" Mandie asked.

"Why, yes, dear, it is," Mrs. Taft agreed.

Stepping back, Mandie admired the ruby-encrusted necklace around her grandmother's neck. "Grandmother, is that a real ruby?" she asked.

"Of course, dear." Mrs. Taft stood and smiled at the senator and Jonathan, who had come in with Celia just in time to hear their conversation.

As Mrs. Taft greeted the senator, Mandie and Celia exchanged glances.

Mandie whispered to her friend, "It sure looks like that ruby that was stolen from the catacombs." She laughed softly. "Of course, I know it's not."

Jonathan apparently overheard her remark. "Sure," he teased, "your grandmother stole the ruby and had it made into a necklace that fast!"

"Oh, Jonathan, I know it's not the same one," Mandie said sharply. "I said it *looks* the same!"

Senator Morton opened the door to the hall. "Ready?" he asked.

"We are now," Mrs. Taft replied. "Come on, dears," she urged the young people.

As they rode down in the lift, Senator Morton suggested, "If it is agreeable with all of you, we thought we'd visit the Fountain of Trevi this morning and the Sistine Chapel this afternoon."

Everyone agreed.

As the *Fontana de Trevi** came within sight, the girls

---

*Fountain of Trevi

gasped in wonder at the huge body of water and the front of the magnificent building behind it. The carriage stopped to let them out.

Mandie and Celia rushed to the rim to look down into the fountain. Water spouted from every statue and stone decoration around it.

As Senator Morton came up behind her, Mandie turned to him. "How old is this?" she asked.

"I believe it was built about 1735," he replied.

"Then it's not really old compared with other landmarks we've seen," Mandie said. The breeze from all the rushing water stirred a strand of hair from under her bonnet.

Jonathan reminded her, "But don't forget the old saying that if you want to return to Rome someday, you should throw a coin into the water and make a wish. Then you'll probably come back."

Mandie and Celia hastily dug into their bags for coins. Mandie put Snowball down on his leash as she tried to find a coin. She didn't have one, only bills. Looking up at Jonathan in disappointment, she said, "I don't have a coin. Could I throw paper money in there?"

"Paper money wouldn't go to the bottom," Jonathan told her.

Senator Morton held out a handful of coins. "Here, take these."

Mandie hesitated. "But if I throw *your* coins in, you will be the one to come back." She laughed. "I have to have my own coins." She thought a moment. "I know. You take this paper bill for a coin." She offered him a lire note.

"If you insist," the senator said, smiling. He accepted the paper money and deposited several coins in Mandie's hand.

"Thank you," Mandie said. Turning back to the edge of the fountain, she spoke thoughtfully, "Now I have to think of a wish." She gazed silently into the pool of water.

"You have to turn around and throw it over your shoulder like this," Jonathan told her, tossing his coin into the water.

The girls watched. Mandie silently made her wish and threw all her coins into the water.

"Mandie, you only have to throw in one coin," Jonathan said.

"I made a wish for each coin, so I had to throw them all in," Mandie said with a shrug and a smile. "Anyway, I don't really believe all this."

"I never thought about doing that," Jonathan said, tossing all his coins into the fountain.

Celia studied the coins in her hand. "There are so many things I'd like to wish for, I don't know exactly which ones to pick," she said. "I suppose the best one would be to wish to come back to Rome, and—"

Jonathan interrupted. "You aren't supposed to tell what your wish is."

Celia looked crestfallen. She quickly threw all the coins into the fountain. "I'll just wish for several things besides that," she said.

As Mandie stood there between her two friends, she said, "I hope someday the three of us will be able to come back to Rome together. I've had such a wonderful time."

"Me, too," Celia agreed.

"You never can tell," Jonathan said lightly. He reached to stick his hand in the water spouting out of a nearby statue.

Mrs. Taft rose from where she was sitting on a nearby bench and came to speak to the young people. "This area has a lot of shops. I thought maybe y'all might want to look around to see if there is something you'd like to buy," she told them.

"And there are sidewalk cafes where we can get something to eat later," the senator added.

"Oh, yes, Grandmother," Mandie said. "I have some money that Celia gave me, and I want to buy something special with it."

"Celia gave you money?" her grandmother asked.

"Yes, ma'am," Mandie replied. "When I lost my bag. Now that I got the bag back, I have that money too."

"But, Celia," Mrs. Taft said, "that wasn't necessary. I am holding money that belongs to Mandie."

"I know, Mrs. Taft," Celia said, dropping her gaze. "I just wanted to give Mandie something."

"I'll buy something for Celia, too, Grandmother," Mandie said.

Senator Morton, hearing their conversation, spoke to Jonathan, "If you want to do any shopping, I can settle up with your father later."

"Thank you, sir, but you've already paid for my new clothes," Jonathan said. "That was the most important to me. And I still have some money left over from yesterday."

The group moved away from the fountain, and as they strolled along, they found dozens of vendors' stalls, displaying everything imaginable. The local craftspeople were selling handmade articles of silk and lace, leather goods, ceramics, and articles made of tortoiseshell and raffia.

Mandie's eyes grew wide as she stopped in front of a collection of cameo brooches. "Look, Celia!" she told her friend. "Would you like one of these?"

Celia looked at the rows and rows of jewelry. "I think the cameos are the prettiest and the most practical," she decided, opening her bag. "I'll buy one."

"No!" Mandie said quickly, drawing money from her bag. "I saw them first, and I'm going to buy one for you and one for me."

Celia looked at her friend. "All right, but I'm going to buy something for you, too."

The owner of the stall did not speak English, but between Senator Morton and Jonathan, they finally figured out how much money the man wanted.

"*Signorina*." The man smiled and handed Mandie the two brooches. "*Grazie*. Thank you."

"Thank *you*," Mandie replied, smiling up at the big Italian man. She turned to Celia and gave her one of the brooches.

"Why don't we wear them now?" Celia said, fastening hers to the neck of her dress.

"Good idea," Mandie agreed.

"Thank you, Mandie," Celia said. "I'll always treasure this. I'll show it to my grandchildren one day and tell them all about you."

Mandie smiled. "I'll always keep mine, too," she said.

"Now it's my turn to buy you something," Celia told her as they followed the adults through the market.

Jonathan tagged along behind them, showing little interest.

"Oh, look at the beautiful combs!" Mandie exclaimed as they passed another stall.

Mrs. Taft heard Mandie and turned around. "What about one for your mother, Amanda?"

"The very thing! One of those tortoiseshell combs

with the diamonds in it," Mandie replied, looking at the colorful array.

"They couldn't possibly be real diamonds, dear, but they are beautiful," her grandmother explained. "I think your mother would like one of those."

Mandie and Celia both bought combs for their mothers. Then Mandie found tiepins and got one for her Uncle John.

"Mandie, how would you like one of these?" Celia asked as she caught sight of a table full of brightly colored scarves.

"Oh, yes, Celia, that would be nice," Mandie said. They stopped in front of the display. "I'd like a red one."

Celia bought two red scarves alike, one for Mandie and one for herself. "We're going to be twins—the same brooches and the same scarves," Celia said, laughing. She handed the scarf to Mandie. "You don't have to wear it today. It's too warm. Just put it in your bag."

"Thank you, Celia," Mandie said. "I really like it. It's something I'll always use and keep." She tucked the silk scarf into her bag.

When it was time for the midday meal, they stopped at a sidewalk cafe and had a light snack. Whenever they ate outdoors, Mandie enjoyed watching the people as they passed by.

When they were finished, Mrs. Taft decided they should go on to the Sistine Chapel.

As they rode in the carriage, Senator Morton explained what they were about to see. "The Sistine Chapel was built in 1470," he told them. "The paintings in it were begun in 1481, or thereabouts, and were done by various well-known artists."

"How do you know all the dates, Senator Morton?" Celia asked.

"Oh, I just read about the Sistine Chapel this morning before we left," he admitted. He continued his explanation: "The paintings, or frescoes, as they are called, represent the life of Moses from the Old Testament on one wall and the life of Christ from the New Testament on the opposite wall."

"It sounds so interesting," Mandie said thoughtfully.

"Wait till you see it," Jonathan told the girls. "You'll always remember it, I'm sure."

When they entered the Sistine Chapel soon thereafter, the girls were speechless as they viewed the artwork. There was the baptism of Christ portrayed, with John the Baptist, the story of Moses, the temptation of Christ, the purification of a leper, the Red Sea, the calling of the apostles, God giving Moses the Tablets of the Law, the Sermon on the Mount, and many, many others. They all stopped before The Last Supper by Rosselli.

"The Italians have so much religious heritage," Mandie remarked as they viewed the painting of Christ at the supper table with His disciples.

"Now look up at the ceiling," Senator Morton told them, pointing above. "It took Michelangelo four years to do the art on this ceiling, and twenty-three years later he painted the Last Judgment. That took him about six years."

The young people stood in silence, gazing at the scenes portrayed.

"That's Christ in the center with His right hand raised," Jonathan told the girls. "The others are the prophets, apostles and martyrs. The good are standing on his right and the sinners are on the left."

The girls gasped in amazement as the painting came alive for them.

"And that must be the resurrection of the dead," Mandie whispered, moving along as she looked overhead.

"Look, the angels are holding the Book of Judgment," Celia added.

Mrs. Taft and Senator Morton followed as the young people roamed the chapel and excitedly discussed its treasures. But finally everyone was tired. Mrs. Taft decided they should all return to the hotel and rest awhile before dinner.

The girls didn't stop talking for a moment all the way back in the carriage. They were so enthused with the city of Rome.

Mrs. Taft led the way into the lobby of the hotel. As they walked past the front desk, the clerk cleared his throat.

"Signorina Shaw," he called.

The whole group stopped to see what he wanted.

The clerk reached under the counter and came up with Mandie's old bag. "Signor Rushton tells me to give this back to you." He handed her the bag.

Mandie took it and looked it over. Holding it up, she said to the others, "Mr. Rushton's maid did a good job of cleaning this. It looks almost like new."

"Yes, dear, it does," Mrs. Taft said. "Let's go to our rooms now."

"Thank you," Mandie called back to the clerk.

He smiled at her, and Mandie hurried along with the others down the corridor.

Once they were alone in their bedroom, the girls quickly changed into their robes. Snowball curled up on the bed and went to sleep.

Mandie picked up her old bag from the table and sat on the edge of the bed. "I'll have to thank Mr. Rushton for getting this cleaned for me," she said. "I don't know when I'll see him, but, come to think of it, he hasn't let us know when he'll be performing here at the hotel."

"I imagine he will," Celia said. She flopped down on the bed. "Mandie, we can't write in our journals, because we don't have the keys to our trunks. There is so much I'd like to write about today."

"We can't disturb Grandmother right now. We'll get the keys later," Mandie promised. "My head is spinning with all we've seen today. Let's take a little nap."

"Shall I pull the draperies to cut out the sunlight?" Celia asked, getting up and going toward the windows.

"Yes," Mandie said. "I'll help you." She went to another window and started to draw the heavy curtains. "Celia, look! My trunk is unlocked!" She stooped to examine it.

Celia glanced at it and then rushed to hers. It was also unlocked.

"How could anyone unlock our trunks when Grandmother has the only keys?" Mandie pondered. She sifted through the contents. "I don't think anything is missing."

"My things are all here, too," Celia said, standing up.

Mandie sat on the floor. "I don't understand what's going on," she said. "If someone went to all the trouble of unlocking our trunks, why didn't they take anything?"

"It's a puzzle to me," Celia replied, joining Mandie on the carpet.

"Celia, do you suppose that strange woman has been in our room?" Mandie asked thoughtfully.

"Oh, Mandie, I hope not," Celia replied. "But I suppose we'd better tell your grandmother about this."

"Well, I don't know," Mandie answered, rising from the floor. "There's nothing missing. And it would only upset her. We can't disturb her right now anyway. Let's take a nap and talk about it later."

Chapter 9 / What Was "It"?

After a short nap, the girls got ready for dinner. While they were dressing, they discussed the unlocked trunks.

"Do you think my grandmother could have unlocked the trunks for some reason?" Mandie asked as she tied a wide ribbon sash around her waist. Before Celia could reply, she added, "No, that couldn't be possible. Grandmother has been with us ever since we locked the trunks this morning."

Celia tried to get her hair to stay up. She used all the combs she could find. "Mandie, I just haven't learned the trick of putting hair up," she moaned. In frustration she removed the combs and brushed her hair out, then started all over again.

"Neither have I," Mandie said as she began pinning up her long blond tresses. But she couldn't get her mind off the mystery of the trunks. "I haven't decided whether to tell Grandmother about the locks on our trunks being opened or not."

Once more Celia failed to get her hair to stay up. "Oh, well," she sighed. "I'll just let my hair hang loose tonight.

It needs washing, and I don't have time to do it." She quickly pulled out the combs and again brushed out her long auburn curls. Then she tied a ribbon in her hair.

"Me, too," Mandie said, letting her hair fall around her shoulders. "This is tiresome work. I don't think it's worth the trouble. For tonight I'll just use the comb that I bought for my mother in my hair."

"You know, Mandie ... about those trunks ..." Celia straightened the bow in her hair. "I think it had to be someone besides your grandmother who got into them."

"I can't figure out how it happened," Mandie said. "I'm sure I locked mine, aren't you?"

"Oh, I'm sure. I even tried the lock after I shut the trunk," Celia replied, going to sit on the side of the bed.

Mandie picked up her old bag and looked at it. "I could use this bag tonight. It looks all right." She hesitated. "Oh, I don't know. I suppose I'll take the one I already have my things in." She put the old bag back on the table near the bed.

Mrs. Taft knocked on their bedroom door and then opened it. "Time to dress, dears," she said, looking into the room. "Goodness, you two seem to be ahead of me all the time lately."

The girls laughed and followed her into the parlor.

"Grandmother, I need to talk to you about—" Mandie began, with the intention of telling her grandmother about the unlocked trunks.

Mrs. Taft cut her short. "Not right now, dear. I must finish getting dressed. I'll be ready shortly." She went back into her bedroom and shut the door.

Mandie looked at Celia. "I've decided to tell her about our trunks."

"I think you ought to," Celia agreed.

But when Mandie once more tried to talk to her grand-mother, she was told, "Later, dear," and they all went downstairs to the hotel dining room for dinner.

Mandie tethered Snowball to the table leg again so that he could eat with them.

"We will be leaving Italy the day after tomorrow," Mrs. Taft told the young people during dinner. "We'll go on over into Switzerland."

"That sounds exciting, but I just love Rome," Mandie remarked as she ate her salad. "I hate to leave."

Celia took a sip of tea. "So do I, but I am anxious to see other countries, too," she added.

"We could stay here a year and never see everything," Jonathan told them. "I've gone to school in Switzerland, but I'm glad I can go back as a tourist and see everything again."

Senator Morton told them, "We won't be staying in a hotel there, you know. We have the use of a friend's chalet."

"Chalet?" Mandie questioned. "Oh, a house."

"Exactly," the senator replied, smiling at her.

"That will be a lot of fun, staying in a real house instead of a stuffy old hotel," Mandie said excitedly.

"Especially when domestic help is furnished with the chalet," Mrs. Taft said.

George Rushton came into the dining room, and seeing Mandie and her friends, he came over to the table to speak to them. There was a taller man with him, but the man walked across the room to sit at a table evidently reserved for them.

"Hello, everyone," Mr. Rushton greeted them.

They all returned the greeting.

But before anyone could say anything else, Mandie

said, "I want to thank you for having your maid clean my bag. It looks almost new again. I really appreciate it."

"I thought she did a good job." He winked at Mandie, then turned to Mrs. Taft and said, "I had told the youngsters that I would be having a performance here at the hotel some night. It's set for tomorrow in the concert room, and I'd like all of you to come as my guests."

"Why, thank you, Mr. Rushton," Mrs. Taft replied, smiling up at him. "We are very grateful for the invitation. However, the senator and I have already made plans to have dinner at a friend's house tomorrow night."

"Does that include Celia and Jonathan and me, Grandmother?" Mandie quickly asked.

Mrs. Taft smiled at her. "No, dear, in fact we were trying to think of something interesting for you young people to do while we are out," she replied.

"Then couldn't we go to Mr. Rushton's performance? Please, Grandmother?" Mandie begged.

Mrs. Taft considered the request for a moment.

Senator Morton spoke up: "I'm sure they would be all right here in the hotel. We could be back before Mr. Rushton's performance is over. And they would be in the company of other people."

"I suppose it would be all right," Mrs. Taft finally agreed. Turning back to Mr. Rushton, she added, "We just don't want to take any chances, leaving them without supervision."

The magician smiled. "I promise to keep an eye on them while I go through my act," he said. "Thank you for letting them attend." He turned to the young people. "Then I'll see you three right after dinner tomorrow night in the concert room." He nodded and went to join his friend at the table across the room.

"I do hope I'm not making a mistake by allowing y'all to go without us," Mrs. Taft said. "Our time is getting short here in Rome, and I had promised a dear friend that we would come to dinner sometime before we left. But since it's an all-adult dinner, you young people wouldn't be able to go with us."

"Don't worry, Grandmother," Mandie told her. "We'll be all right."

"But you remember what happened when we left y'all in a hotel in Paris," Mrs. Taft reminded them.

"We won't get separated this time," Jonathan promised.

"I'm going to be awfully strict about this," Mrs. Taft told them as she looked around the table. "You are not to go anywhere else or even speak to anyone else. And you are to stay in the concert room until we come for you. Is that clear?"

"Yes, ma'am," the three replied.

Mandie smiled. "Thank you for letting us go, Grandmother," she said.

"Are you sure you want to go?" Mrs. Taft asked. "After all, you have seen Mr. Rushton do his tricks. I don't know what could be different this time."

"Oh, yes," Mandie replied eagerly. She looked at her friends for confirmation.

"Yes, ma'am," Celia added.

"I don't know of anything better to do, so I'll go along with the girls," Jonathan teased.

Mandie frowned playfully. "Oh, really, Jonathan Guyer," she said sternly. Then she burst into laughter.

"What's so funny?" Jonathan asked solemnly.

"You are," Mandie replied, still laughing. "I know

you're anxious to see how he does his tricks, but you won't admit it."

"All right, after you've seen him do his magic again, I'll wager you will have caught on to some of his tricks," Jonathan replied.

"If I do, you'll be the first to know," Mandie promised.

Mrs. Taft told them, "Please hurry now and finish so we'll have time for a stroll before we retire for the night."

As the group walked around the square near the hotel, people stopped to look at Snowball parading along at the end of his leash. Then suddenly the kitten came face to face with a white, woolly poodle—also at the end of a leash. Holding the leash was an exquisitely dressed older woman who was accompanied by a young man.

Snowball stopped in his tracks. But the poodle kept walking along in his direction. Mandie started to pick up her kitten when Snowball decided to attack. He lunged forward into the poodle's face. The leash slipped out of Mandie's hand. The poodle was so surprised he just stood there as the white kitten spit at him and boxed him with his paws.

Mrs. Taft gasped, "Amanda!"

Jonathan quickly bent to pick up Snowball, but the kitten tried to claw him. Mandie stooped and slapped Snowball's paws as she picked him up. The young man grabbed the white poodle.

"I'm very sorry," Mandie told him.

The young man was tall and muscular with a ruddy complexion and eyes almost as blue as Mandie's. "We are sorry, too," he replied. "Where we come from cats do not attack dogs." He laughed.

"They don't where we come from either, that is, except for Snowball. He'll attack anything," Mandie told him.

Mrs. Taft apologized to the woman, who didn't seem to understand a word that was being said. The woman chattered away in a language Mandie had never heard before. The young man translated.

"My grandmother apologizes, also," he said to Mrs. Taft. "She would like to give you a ride in her new motor car to wherever you are going."

"Motor car!" Mandie and Celia exclaimed.

Mrs. Taft was equally surprised. "Oh my, she has a motor car?"

"Yes, it's sitting just around the corner," he said, pointing in the general direction.

"I have never ridden in one," Mrs. Taft told the young man.

"We would be pleased to have you travel in ours then," he replied.

Senator Morton encouraged Mrs. Taft, "Now would be a good time to try it out. You've said that perhaps you'd purchase one someday."

Mandie and Celia were speechless. Mandie could only think of the awful noise the cars made. The few she had seen seemed to jerk and start erratically. She wasn't sure she wanted to ride in one.

"They're a lot of fun," Jonathan remarked to the girls.

The young man and his grandmother conversed in their language for a moment, and then he spoke again to Mrs. Taft in English: "My grandmother would like to introduce herself to you. She is the Baroness Hildegard Geissler, and I am Rupert Geissler. We are from Germany."

Mrs. Taft gasped, then at once composed herself as she looked the woman over. The baroness, too, was tall and strong-looking, with the same coloring as her grandson. "Did you say your grandmother is a baroness?" Mrs. Taft asked.

"Yes, that's right," Rupert said with a smile.

"Please introduce us to her. I am Mrs. Norman Taft. This is my granddaughter, Amanda Shaw, and her friends Celia Hamilton and Jonathan Guyer." Then turning with obvious respect to the senator, she said, "And this is Senator Morton of the United States Senate in Washington, D.C. We are Americans. We are pleased to make your acquaintance."

As Rupert translated, his grandmother smiled and then spoke rapidly. He spoke to Mrs. Taft again, "My grandmother says to tell you that her daughter, my mother, is married to an American and living in New York," he explained. "She also says, now that we are properly introduced, would you care to take a ride in her motor car?"

Snowball struggled in Mandie's arms and hissed menacingly at the white poodle Rupert was holding. She had to hold him tight.

"Grandmother," Mandie said, "I don't think it would work to get into a motor car with Snowball and the poodle, too. I could take Snowball and walk back to the hotel while you ride in it," she offered.

Jonathan reached for the kitten. "I'll take Snowball, Mandie. I've ridden in motor cars lots of times. You haven't."

"And I will walk back with Jonathan," Senator Morton volunteered. "I have ridden in motor cars before, too."

Mandie held on to her kitten, and both girls waited silently for Mrs. Taft to instruct them how to proceed.

"Please thank your grandmother," she told Rupert. "And tell her we will be happy to ride back to the hotel in your motor car. However, our hotel is only four or five blocks back that way." She pointed in the direction they had come.

Rupert told his grandmother and then said to Mrs. Taft and the girls, "If you will, please follow us."

Mandie finally gave Jonathan her kitten. "Please pray for us to get safely back to the hotel," she said.

Jonathan smiled his mischievous smile as he took the cat. "You'll get back all right. It's not that dangerous."

"Sounds dangerous to me," Celia finally spoke.

"You don't have to go, Celia," Mrs. Taft told her. "You may walk back with Jonathan and the senator if you wish."

Mandie looked at her friend.

Celia took Mandie's hand and said, "Thank you, Mrs. Taft, but if Mandie is going, then I'll go too. That's what friends are for—times like these."

Mrs. Taft smiled at her, and the young man led the way down the street. Senator Morton and Jonathan went the other way with Snowball.

The motor car was parked under some trees on the next street. The car was fancier than any Mandie had seen before. There were a lot of shiny accessories on it and no visible top.

As they stood in awe surveying the vehicle, Mandie asked, "Who is going to drive it?"

"I am," Rupert told her as he helped his grandmother and Mrs. Taft into the small rear seat. Then he turned to help the girls squeeze into the narrow front seat with him.

The girls held their breath. When Rupert got the car going, they held hands and softly repeated their verse: "What time I am afraid I will put my trust in Thee." No one seemed to hear them over the roar of the racing motor.

To their amazement, the car did not jerk or rattle, as they expected it would, but sailed smoothly forward. The girls kept their eyes shut during the short trip, and in a few minutes Rupert pulled up in front of their hotel, and tooted the car's horn to announce their arrival.

"Here we are," he said. He helped the girls out and then assisted the ladies from the vehicle.

Mrs. Taft thanked the baroness and asked Rupert to tell his grandmother that they would be going to Germany before leaving Europe.

The baroness insisted that they come to visit her. She and Rupert would be home by the time Mrs. Taft and her group arrived in Germany, they said.

Senator Morton and Jonathan walked up in front of the hotel.

As the Geisslers drove off, Mrs. Taft watched them. "Yes, yes, I must have one of those motor cars," she told the senator.

"But, Grandmother," Mandie said, "you won't get rid of Ben and the rig, will you? Celia and I love to ride in it." Still nervous from the ride, she wasn't sure that she ever wanted to go anyplace in another motor car.

"No, of course not, Amanda," Mrs. Taft assured her as they all entered the hotel.

Mrs. Taft didn't stop talking all the way to the elevator and up to their rooms. Mandie knew how much her grandmother loved to socialize with royalty and important government figures. She also knew they would eventually visit the baroness and her grandson.

Once they were in their room and had dressed for the night, the girls sat on the bed discussing the events of the evening. Snowball had already curled up in a ball and was sound asleep.

"How did you like the ride?" Mandie asked her friend.

"I didn't like it one bit. I was absolutely terrified," Celia admitted.

"But you didn't say anything," Mandie said.

"Because I didn't want your grandmother to know how scared I was," Celia answered. "I know you were afraid, too, Mandie. Otherwise we wouldn't have said our verse, right?"

Mandie nodded. "If we go to visit the baroness in Germany—I should say *when* we go, because I know my grandmother likes to associate with people like that—I don't think I'll ride in her motor car," Mandie declared. "It was scary for me, too."

"Our journals, Mandie," Celia reminded her, getting up to fetch hers from her trunk. She returned to the bed with the book and a pencil.

Mandie jumped off the bed. "Yes, we have to write about this in our journals," she agreed. She got hers and went to sit in a big chair to write.

Celia looked up from her journal. "Mandie, you never did tell your grandmother about our trunks being unlocked," she reminded her friend.

"I know. I never could seem to get her attention," Mandie said. "But I suppose now I shouldn't tell her. She probably wouldn't leave us here in the hotel tomorrow night, even though we're going to Mr. Rushton's performance."

"But after that, we'd better tell her," Celia suggested.

"I will if I can get her to listen to me," Mandie agreed, writing rapidly in her journal.

When the girls finally crawled into bed, they were exhausted and soon fell asleep.

Mandie dreamed about the motor car. Somehow her mother and her baby brother, Samuel, were riding in it with her. There didn't seem to be a driver, and the vehicle was flying through the streets of Rome. She could hear the horn tooting by itself. The faster it went the more out of breath she became. Suddenly she awoke with a start.

Trying to quiet her racing heartbeat, Mandie took a few deep breaths and stared at the ceiling in the faint light from outside. All at once she heard a slight noise as though something had been torn. She listened carefully, and as she turned in the bed, she saw a shadow on the wall by the bureau. Someone was in the room!

Stifling a scream, she nudged Celia and whispered in her ear, "Don't move." She grabbed her friend's hand.

As they lay there, holding hands, Mandie could feel Celia trembling. Mandie tried to see what the shadow was doing but couldn't. She glanced down at the foot of the bed. Snowball was not there.

Just then Snowball let out an angry wail. The intruder had apparently stepped on the kitten. The shadow quickly stepped aside.

Mandie sat upright. "What do you want?" she shouted.

Celia sat up, too.

The shadow moved slightly.

Mandie jumped out of bed. "Who are you?" she demanded.

"What did you do with it?" the voice was gruff, and Mandie couldn't tell whether the intruder was a man or a woman.

At that moment Celia let out an ear-splitting scream and disappeared under the covers. The shadow quickly moved to the French door that led outside.

Mandie screamed and raced across the room in time to see the shadow disappear through the doorway.

Mrs. Taft came running into the room, dressed in her robe and nightgown. Senator Morton and Jonathan were close behind.

"What on earth is going on?" Mrs. Taft asked. She switched on an electric lamp and looked around the room.

"We heard someone scream clear across the hall," Senator Morton said.

Mandie's heart was pounding, and she could hardly speak. "Grandmother—someone was in here—just now," she said. "Whoever it was—" She turned to see what interested the intruder at their bureau. "Look!" She held up her old purse. "They tore up my bag!"

"Are you or Celia hurt?" Mrs. Taft looked anxiously at Celia, who was still cowering under the bed covers.

"No, ma'am," Mandie shook her head. "We were just frightened."

Senator Morton checked the French door and found it unlocked. There was a key in the lock, and he turned that, then pulled the draperies over it. "Maybe I should go down to the desk and report this," he said turning to Mrs. Taft.

"Oh, I don't know, Senator, whoever it was is gone now," Mrs. Taft said, obviously shaken. "Why don't we notify the hotel clerk in the morning."

"If you girls are afraid, I'll be glad to sleep on the sofa in the parlor," Jonathan offered.

"No, but thanks anyway, Jonathan," Mandie said.

"Could we leave the light on the rest of the night?" Celia asked nervously, peeking out from the covers.

Mrs. Taft went over to comfort the girl. "I'll tell you what, dear," Mrs. Taft said. "We'll leave both bedroom doors open and the light on in the parlor. Will that be all right?"

"Yes, ma'am," Celia replied. "Thank you."

After everyone said good night and the others went to their rooms, Mandie and Celia huddled together in the big bed. The faint light from the parlor lamp was a small comfort.

But Mandie couldn't go to sleep right away. She kept wondering why anyone would tear up her old purse. If the intruder were trying to rob them, he—or she—would surely have taken the bag that had something in it. Celia's bag was also on the bureau, in plain view.

What was it the intruder had said? "What did you do with it?"

Mandie couldn't figure out what "it" was.

Chapter 10 / Hired Protection

Everyone was tired and groggy the next morning. When the maid came with the breakfast trays, Mrs. Taft had her place them on a table in the parlor and she and the girls sat and ate there together.

"Amanda, dear, I'm wondering whether we should leave Italy today," she said. "After last night, I'm puzzled and concerned about what they were after, whoever it was."

"I don't know, either, Grandmother," Mandie replied. "I can't imagine why someone would come into our room and tear up my old purse with nothing in it."

"If we hadn't screamed, there's no telling what they might have done," Celia added.

"As soon as I get dressed, I'll ask Senator Morton to go downstairs with me, and we'll talk to the manager," Mrs. Taft promised.

Mandie was so upset about the intruder that she completely forgot to tell her grandmother about their trunks being unlocked.

When they were finished with their food, Mrs. Taft told the girls to get dressed quickly. She would ask Jonathan to stay in the parlor with them while she and the senator went downstairs.

The girls looked through the clothes in their wardrobe. "I'm going to wear this older dark blue dress since I don't know what we'll be doing yet," Mandie said. "And I think I'll plait my hair today."

"And I'll wear my brown dress," Celia decided. "I don't care for it on me, but my mother likes it. I'll tie my hair back with a bright ribbon, maybe yellow. What do you think, Mandie?"

"Sounds fine, Celia," she answered. After they had dressed, Mandie and Celia stood before the floor-length mirror. They both giggled at once.

"We look like schoolgirls again!" Mandie exclaimed. "And we've been trying to look so grown up."

"But we do look like proper young ladies, even if it is younger ladies than we'd like to be," Celia added with a giggle.

When Mrs. Taft brought Jonathan in to stay with the girls, he looked from one to the other and smiled his mischievous smile. "That fright last night must have caused you two to lose a couple of years," he teased.

"Jonathan! We're only trying to look like nice young girls today," Mandie protested. "I see you're also wearing darker clothes than usual. That dark gray does make you look very intelligent, whether or not you are."

Jonathan shook his head and laughed at Mandie.

"After what happened to us last night," Celia said, "We're not in a teasing mood this morning."

Jonathan looked concerned. "I'm sorry girls. I really am. I know it must have been terribly frightening to wake up in the night and find someone in the room with you," he said.

"Do you think it could have been that strange woman from the ship?" Celia asked.

"I don't know," Mandie said. "In fact I can't figure out the whole situation. Why would anyone go to the trouble to break into our room just to tear up my old bag?"

"Well, come to think of it, your bag *has* had some mystery attached to it," Jonathan told her. "First, it disappeared at the catacombs, and then it turned up anonymously on the front desk down in the lobby. Why would anyone steal it and then return it?"

"Celia may be right. That strange woman may have had something to do with it. We did see her at the catacombs, you know," Mandie reminded him. "And for some reason she always tries to avoid us."

In a few minutes Mrs. Taft came back alone. Hurrying into the parlor, she thanked Jonathan for staying with the girls and sat down near the door. "Senator Morton has gone to engage the services of a private detective for the rest of our stay here in Italy," she told the young people.

"A private detective!" Mandie exclaimed.

"A real one?" Jonathan asked.

"Yes, a real private detective," Mrs. Taft replied. "The manager recommended one who speaks English, and the senator has gone to talk with him. Of course, the manager apologized for what happened last night. He'll have that outside door to your room sealed up today after we go out."

"Did you report it to the police, Grandmother?" Mandie asked.

"No, dear," Mrs. Taft replied. "The senator and I talked it over, and since we want to leave Italy by tomorrow, we thought it best not to become involved in legal technicalities which might delay us."

"Where are we going today, Mrs. Taft?" Jonathan asked.

"Well, I thought we could get a carriage and just ride around the city to no place in particular," she said.

"And just stop whenever we like?" Mandie added.

"Sounds great to me," Jonathan said.

"I think that would be very relaxing after such a terrible night," Celia agreed. "I just don't have much energy or enthusiasm today."

When Senator Morton came in a few minutes later, a huge man was with him. The senator introduced him, "Mrs. Taft, this is Mr. John Swaggingham."

The detective bowed slightly and greeted Mandie's grandmother warmly. He was not only big around but awfully tall. He was a friendly, middle-aged man with curly brown hair and a darker mustache. When he spoke, Mandie decided he was British.

Hearing the man's name, Mandie turned her head to hide her smile. He did swagger slightly when he walked. And he was so big! As they all sat down in the parlor, Mandie noticed that the detective was bigger than the chair.

The young people were introduced, and Mandie liked the detective immediately. Jonathan and Celia seemed to like him, too.

"Mr. Swaggingham has agreed to accompany us for the rest of our stay here in Italy," Senator Morton explained. "Of course I told him about last night, and he will sleep on the sofa here in the parlor tonight. We'll be leaving tomorrow."

"We appreciate your help, Mr. Swaggingham," Mrs. Taft told him. "We're all going to feel safer with you around."

"Thank you, madam," the detective replied. "It will be my pleasure to be in the company of such lovely ladies." He glanced over to include Mandie and Celia.

Mandie suddenly had an idea. "Can you catch people who try to get away?" she asked. "I mean, suppose I kept seeing someone, and every time I tried to catch the person, they disappeared? Just supposing, of course."

Celia and Jonathan quickly glanced at Mandie.

"Yes, Miss, I probably could," the man assured her. "I know I look big and clumsy, but I get about rather quickly when necessary. I lose very few indeed."

Mrs. Taft stood up. "I think we'd better get going if we want some time to sightsee before the noon meal," she said.

As they all prepared to leave the suite, Mr. Swaggingham instructed them to stay together and near him since he couldn't very well keep track of them in five different directions.

Mandie and Celia trailed behind to whisper. "I guess we'll have to go to restrooms to talk, if we don't want him to overhear everything we say," Mandie told Celia.

They walked toward the hired carriage in front of the hotel.

"But that means we can't talk to Jonathan without the detective hearing," Celia whispered back.

Jonathan looked at the girls curiously and smiled his mischievous smile. "I know what you're talking about," he teased in a whisper.

"No, you don't," Mandie replied.

"You were trying to figure out how we're going to talk privately with him around," Jonathan said softly.

The girls smiled at him and climbed into the carriage. But it didn't turn out to be much of a problem after all.

As the carriage driver took them up one street and down the next so they could see most of the city, Mr. Swaggingham carried on a conversation with Senator Morton and Mrs. Taft most of the time. He didn't seem to notice what the young people did or said. Now and then they all stopped to look at some historical landmark, and at noon they ate at a sidewalk cafe.

At one of the last sites they stopped to visit, Senator Morton spoke to Jonathan, "I suppose I'd better go by the telegraph office and wire your father," he said. "I need to give him the address where we'll be staying in Switzerland so he'll know where you are."

"Thank you, sir," Jonathan said. "I appreciate your going to so much trouble for me."

"No trouble," the senator replied. "We're lucky to have you along to help entertain these two young ladies." He winked at Mandie and Celia.

"Yes, Jonathan, we really appreciate your being with us," Mandie told him.

"We trust you can stay with us the rest of the time we're in Europe," Mrs. Taft said, finishing her cup of tea.

"I'm so glad we met up with you, Jonathan," Celia added.

"Well, you all flatter me," Jonathan said, blushing slightly.

"I'll also check while I'm there to see if any message has been received from your aunt and uncle in Paris," Senator Morton added.

"I do wish I could hear from them," Jonathan replied. "I hope I can stay with them when you people go back home."

"It would be nice if we could meet them before we leave Europe," Mrs. Taft said.

Senator Morton explained the situation to Mr. Swaggingham, "Jonathan's aunt and uncle are newspaper people in Paris, and they've been away on an assignment ever since we got to Europe."

"They are French?" the detective asked.

"Oh, no, they're from the United States," the senator told him. "They are with a branch of a New York newspaper in Paris."

"I see," the man answered. "Would you like me to locate them for you?"

"That won't be necessary," the senator replied. "You see, we stay in touch with his father in New York. He has asked us to keep Jonathan with us until his relatives do return to Paris or Mr. Buyer comes over here himself."

The detective turned to Jonathan. "You are the son of Jonathan Lindall Guyer, Jr., is that right?" he asked. "I saw the newspaper articles when you ran away from home."

"Yes, sir," Jonathan confirmed.

"I have done work for your father right here in Italy," the detective told him.

"You have?" Jonathan asked in surprise. "What kind of work?"

"Oh, I've checked out a few references on people he does business with and that sort of thing," Mr. Swaggingham said. "Nothing of great importance."

"Any money my father spends is important to him," Jonathan said.

"I know," the detective agreed.

"Well, if you'll sit here with the ladies, I'll get the carriage, and we'll cover a couple more sights before we go back to the hotel," the senator told him.

As soon as Senator Morton returned with the carriage

that had been waiting, they went to the telegraph office. He sent Jonathan's father a message and found that the boy's relatives had not been in contact with him yet, so he relayed another message to the Paris office of the newspaper they worked for, giving the address where they would be staying in Switzerland.

"Now, that's done," the senator said as he returned to the carriage. "Why don't we drive along the Tiber River?"

The others were agreeable, and the driver took them along the river that flows through the city of Rome. Now and then they saw a small boat. And one of them quickly drew Mandie's attention.

"Look! That boat over there!" she said, pointing. "See that woman on it? She's the woman from the ship!"

They all turned to look. The woman didn't seem to be aware of their gaze. The boat was traveling in the same direction they were.

Mrs. Taft shielded her eyes to look across the water. "I do believe it is the same woman," she said.

"Can we ride along the river's edge until her boat docks, and then we could stop, too?" Mandie asked.

"My, no, dear, we can't go chasing that woman," her grandmother said sternly. "There's no telling where she is headed. I wonder if the others in the boat with her are her companions, or just traveling on the same boat."

Mr. Swaggingham listened with interest to the conversation. "That's a public boat," he said, "a ferry that people take for a small fee. It stops at various places along the river."

"It's stopping on the other side, and she's getting off!" Mandie exclaimed as their carriage crept along at a sightseeing pace.

"And we can't drive the carriage across the river, so that's the end of her for now," Jonathan reminded Mandie.

"One of these days!" Mandie muttered, mostly to herself.

Later that afternoon, Mrs. Taft decided they should return to their hotel so the young people could have an early dinner in the dining room. She and the senator were dining at the home of her friend, but she told them they would at least sit with the young people while they had their meal.

"But, madam, that won't be necessary," Mr. Swaggingham told her. "You are paying me to look after the young people. I will be glad to sit with them in the dining room. I can have my dinner at the same time."

"Of course, Mr. Swaggingham," Mrs. Taft said as the carriage drew up in front of the hotel. "I'd forgotten. That will give me time to rest a little before I have to dress for the evening."

As they entered the lobby, the desk clerk stopped Senator Morton. "The door has been sealed in the young ladies' room," he said. "The window on that side also. They should be safe now."

They all thanked him and went up to their rooms. Mr. Swaggingham checked out the door and the window that had been closed up. Everything seemed to be all right, so the young people freshened up for dinner, and Mrs. Taft lay down to rest.

When Jonathan joined them in the parlor, Mandie called through the door to her grandmother's bedroom. "We're going to eat now, Grandmother," she said, picking up Snowball.

"All right, dear. We'll see you before we go, either

down there or up here if you get back before we leave," Mrs. Taft answered through the closed door.

In the dining room a few minutes later, the waiter showed them to a table. Mandie fastened Snowball's leash to the table leg, and they ordered their food. Without the adults to talk with, Mr. Swaggingham was quiet and listened to the young people's conversation as they discussed the extraordinary sights they had seen in Rome.

After they began eating, Mandie asked the detective about the stolen gem at the catacombs. "Do you know if they've found the stone or caught anyone yet?" she asked.

"I don't believe they have," Mr. Swaggingham replied. "It usually takes a long time to solve something like that."

Mandie looked up and saw her grandmother rushing toward them. As Mrs. Taft came up to the table, Mr. Swaggingham and Jonathan stood up.

"Oh, dear, Amanda," Mrs. Taft began. "I can't find my ruby necklace anywhere."

"Your ruby necklace has disappeared?" Mandie was shocked.

Mrs. Taft sat down to talk to her granddaughter. "Do you remember fastening it for me when I wore it the other day, dear?" she asked. "The hook was difficult to work, wasn't it?"

"Yes, Grandmother, I had trouble getting it to fasten," Mandie agreed. "Do you think you might have lost the necklace while you wore it?"

"I just don't know," her grandmother said. "I either lost it or someone has stolen it. I just don't remember taking it off when I undressed."

"Would you like me to search your suite for you?" Mr. Swaggingham offered.

"Would you, please?" Mrs. Taft was frantic. "I've looked everywhere I can think of, but you, being a detective, might have better success than I did."

The young people hurriedly swallowed the last bites of their meal and rose to follow the adults back to the suite. Mandie snatched a piece of meat off the table, quickly covered it with her handkerchief, and picked Snowball up from under the table.

She knew the kitten had not finished what she had given him earlier. Holding him up against her face, she whispered, "Don't worry. I have a piece of chicken for you." He rolled out his rough red tongue and licked her cheek.

As she rode with the others back up in the elevator, she wondered what would happen next. She was sure the ruby necklace was extremely valuable because she remembered asking her grandmother if it were real.

Well, maybe this detective can find it, Mandie thought.

Chapter 11 / A Mystery Solved

Everyone stood by watching while Mr. Swaggingham thoroughly searched Mrs. Taft's room and her belongings. Then he searched the parlor and moved on into the room Mandie and Celia shared. The ruby necklace was not to be found.

Mrs. Taft, nervously overseeing the search, finally sat down on the settee in the parlor and sighed. "I have insurance on it, of course, but that was a family heirloom that I intended passing down to you, Amanda. I can collect the money for it, but that won't replace its value to me."

Mandie sat by her grandmother and held her hand as she looked up into Mrs. Taft's worried face. "Grandmother, please don't worry about it. I know it was valuable, but you know that small, simple things mean more to me, like the rose I pressed from my mother's wedding bouquet when she married Uncle John, and the map we found that showed where Aunt Ruby had hidden her treasure."

Mrs. Taft embraced her granddaughter silently.

"Besides," Mandie reminded her, "we can't take material things with us when we die. You have given me your love, and that's more important than any gift you can ever leave to me, Grandmother."

Mandie moved back from her grandmother's embrace, and saw that tears filled Mrs. Taft's eyes. Mandie squeezed her tight.

Suddenly Snowball jumped into Mandie's lap, startling them both. He began meowing and raised his front paws to his mistress's shoulder.

Mandie gasped. "Snowball!" she scolded.

Mrs. Taft smiled. "Why, I do believe your cat is jealous, Amanda," she said.

"Maybe, but he also knows I have a piece of chicken for him here in my handkerchief," Mandie said, taking the rolled-up cloth from her pocket. She got up and walked toward the bathroom to feed him.

"Amanda! You brought meat from the table in your pocket?" Mrs. Taft exclaimed. She shook her head. "Oh, what you won't do for that cat!"

When Senator Morton came to take Mrs. Taft to her friend's house, she told him about the missing necklace, and he urged her to report it to the police.

"But you know we'd get delayed with police paperwork, and we want to leave tomorrow," she said.

"You could at least report it to the manager of the hotel," Senator Morton advised. "Especially in light of the other things that have been happening."

Mandie suddenly remembered the unlocked trunks.

"Grandmother, I've been trying to tell you something else," Mandie said hurriedly as her grandmother stood at the doorway ready to leave. "Celia and I locked our trunks when we went out yesterday morning, and when we came back they were both unlocked."

"What?" Mrs. Taft turned back into the room. "Amanda! Are you sure?"

"Yes, Grandmother, we are both certain of it," Mandie assured her. "Don't you have all the keys to everything?"

"Well, yes, I do," her grandmother said. "In fact, I've been keeping them in the pocket of my fur cape in the wardrobe, and I just saw them."

"That's an odd place to put keys, isn't it?" Senator Morton said, smiling at Mrs. Taft. "How clever of you. I never would have thought of it, so I suppose thieves wouldn't either."

"Was anything missing, dear?" Mrs. Taft asked Mandie, ignoring the senator's comment. "How about yours, Celia?"

"Nothing," the girls replied.

"All I can say is, I'll be glad when we finally leave this hotel," Mrs. Taft said. She turned toward the door again. "Let's go to that dinner and hurry back before something else happens."

Senator Morton spoke to Mr. Swaggingham. "Please be sure these young people stay within your sight at all times."

"Yes, sir," the detective promised.

When the adults had left, the young people sat in the parlor and discussed the ruby necklace. Mr. Swaggingham sprawled on a chair and listened.

"I remember you saying the ruby in your grandmother's necklace looked similar to the stone that was stolen at the catacombs," Jonathan remarked.

"Well, I don't know much about precious stones, but to me they looked a lot alike," Mandie told him.

"I thought so, too," Celia added. "But I don't see what difference that would make."

Jonathan arched his eyebrows. "Perhaps the thief who stole the gem in the catacombs intended to replace it with the one from your grandmother's necklace," he suggested.

"No, I think that would be too complicated," Mandie disagreed. "Besides, my grandmother wore the necklace yesterday, *after* the other ruby was stolen."

Everyone looked confused.

Mr. Swaggingham straightened up. "It can get complicated when one tries to unravel the doings of thieves," he agreed.

"What do you think the thief will do with the ruby from the catacombs?" Jonathan asked.

"It would be too easily identifiable to sell as it is," Mr. Swagginham explained, "so he probably would have it cut, unless he knew a buyer who would take it as an addition to a collection. The police usually work through both avenues."

"Maybe whoever was in our room last night took my grandmother's necklace," Mandie suggested.

"But your grandmother said she didn't hear anything until we screamed," Celia reminded her.

"The thief most likely took it while we were all gone, that is, if Mrs. Taft didn't just lose it because of the faulty clasp," Jonathan decided.

"You're probably right, Jonathan," Mandie agreed excitedly. "But that must mean he was in our suite three times."

"Why?" Jonathan asked.

"Because we found our trunks unlocked yesterday before the intruder came at night, and Grandmother was wearing her necklace that day," Mandie reasoned. "She didn't find it missing until this afternoon. So if the thief stole the necklace this morning while we were out, that makes three times he *or she* was in our suite."

Mr. Swaggingham laughed heartily and slapped his knee. "You young people can really weave a tale of suspense. I think you ought to write a mystery story. It would really be good."

They all laughed.

Then the detective pulled out a pocket watch on a chain and looked at it. "I believe it's time we went down to the concert room," he remarked, standing up. "Please stay together and within my sight at all times."

The young people promised they would, and they all went downstairs. In spite of Mr. Swaggingham's protests, Mandie insisted on bringing Snowball with her. She was afraid someone would let him out.

People were already seated in the concert room when they entered, but they did manage to find four seats near the front. There was a small stage in the room, and the curtain was closed. A pianist was playing soft music in a corner of the room.

Mandie held Snowball, and sat between her two friends, and Mr. Swaggingham sat on the other side of Jonathan. Mandie was glad that she and Celia could whisper without the detective overhearing them.

"If I can get a chance, I'm going to ask Mr. Rushton if we can see his equipment so Jonathan can show us how it works," Mandie whispered in Celia's ear. "Jonathan said he could do the tricks, too."

"I'd like to know how he does everything," Celia whispered back. "I don't really believe in magic."

"We'll find out whether it's really magic or just some tricks Mr. Rushton knows," Mandie whispered.

The music suddenly became louder, and the curtain

parted. The stage was smaller than the one in the theater, but the magician managed to do exactly the same act he had done in the theater.

Mandie sighed. "Oh, shucks!" she said to her friends. "I thought he'd do something different, but it looks like it's going to be the same old thing we saw before."

She watched closely when George Rushton took an empty case and made a stone appear in it. As he pulled back his handkerchief, revealing a red gem on the black velvet background, Mandie gasped. Her friends turned to her.

During the applause, Mandie explained her reaction. "That wasn't the same stone he used the last time. It was shaped differently. I'm sure of it."

"I think you're right," Jonathan said, "but what difference does it make?"

Mandie glanced over at the detective. He didn't seem to be paying any attention to their conversation. "Maybe none. We'll find out," she said.

The performance was over earlier than the young people had expected.

When the lights came back on in the room and everyone stood up to leave, Mandie spoke to Mr. Swaggingham. "Why don't we go in the dining room and have a cup of tea or something?" she suggested, cuddling Snowball. "It's too early for my grandmother and the senator to get back."

Her friends looked puzzled, but the detective readily agreed with the idea. "I could use a cup of tea. Just see that you stay together in this crowd."

After they were seated for a few minutes in the dining room, Mandie spoke to Celia, "I think I need to find the restroom. Will you come with me?" She stood up, holding Snowball.

Celia joined her and they excused themselves from the table.

"Please be sure to come directly back to the table," the detective cautioned. As the girls started across the dining room, Mandie heard Jonathan say, "I think I'll find the men's room myself."

The detective urged him to hurry back, and Jonathan said he would not be long. Once Mandie was out of Mr. Swaggingham's sight, she watched as Jonathan headed for a door labeled *Il Gabinetto*, which they had learned earlier indicated the restroom.

Mandie caught Jonathan's attention and motioned for him to follow as she and Celia slipped past the door to the women's room and hurried out of the dining room. He caught up with them at the front desk.

"Can you tell us which room Mr. George Rushton is staying in?" Mandie asked the clerk.

The man smiled. "Suite 100, Signorina," he replied.

"What are you girls up to now?' Jonathan asked.

"I thought maybe Mr. Rushton would be in his room by now so we could talk to him and see his equipment," Mandie told him.

"Mandie," Jonathan began, "you know we promised not to get out of the detective's sight."

"It will only be for a few minutes," Mandie argued. She started walking down the long corridor.

"But you lied to Mr. Swaggingham, then, Mandie," Celia said as she followed.

"No, I didn't," Mandie objected. "We will go by the restroom on the way back to the table—after we see Mr. Rushton."

Jonathan stepped in front of Mandie, blocking her way. "I'm beginning to see now what Celia was talking about when she said you were always getting involved in adventures," he said. "But, Mandie, please think about what you're doing this time. There is a real live thief running loose somewhere. It could be dangerous."

"I'm not afraid, Jonathan," Mandie said. "If you are, then you can go on back to the table with Mr. Swaggingham. Celia, you can, too."

Celia shook her head. "It is scary to think about, but I have to come with you, Mandie. I can't let you get into something all by yourself."

"And I suppose I'll have to come along to guard you two stubborn girls," Jonathan teased.

As they began walking again, all three of them saw the strange woman from the ship at once. She was hurrying down the corridor ahead of them.

"Quick!" Mandie said. All three of them raced after the woman. But she was too quick for them. She rushed into the elevator nearby and left the floor.

"Well, there she went again!" Mandie said in exasperation.

"Mandie, don't you think we ought to go back to the table?" Celia asked. "Mr. Swaggingham is probably curious by now as to what we're doing."

"No, I'm going to see Mr. Rushton just for a minute," she said, looking at room numbers along the corridor. She finally spotted Suite 100. "There it is," she said, pointing across the hallway.

Mandie paused to compose herself and to think of exactly what to say to the man if he answered the door. Her friends patiently followed to see what she was going to do.

Slowly approaching the door to Suite 100, Mandie cleared her throat quietly, and raised her hand to knock.

Suddenly, she realized the door was not completely closed.

She stood there, uncertain what to do, when a conversation within the room drifted through the slightly opened door. She put her finger to her lips to caution her friends to be quiet.

A man's voice with a foreign accent was saying, "I did search. In fact, I tore the girl's bag apart. It wasn't in it."

Mandie's heart raced. Someone was talking about her! She looked at Celia and Jonathan, who stuck close by. They opened their eyes wide. They had heard, too.

Mandie recognized George Rushton's voice: "That's your fault. It was your idea—not mine—to sew the gem you took from the catacombs into the girl's purse."

Mandie and her friends held their breath.

"That was the safest way I knew to get it out of the country," the voice with the foreign accent replied. "When I returned the bag to the desk here at the hotel, the stone was tightly concealed in it. And when I got to the girl's room to check on it, it was gone."

"That was a big mistake, roaming around in that girl's room like that," George Rushton told him.

"I had to be sure the clerk gave her the bag and that the gem was still in it," the man explained. "That way I could follow them out of the country and get the bag back again to recover the gem after we crossed the border."

"This is all your problem, not mine," George Rushton replied.

"What do you mean, my problem? It's yours too. You're in this with me," the man said angrily.

"You can't do anything right," George Rushton argued. "You blow out all the candles in the catacombs, and then fail to get the ruby. And then the next day, when you finally get the stone, you steal the girl's bag to put it in and now you tell me the gem is not in the bag!"

Now just a minute," the other man said quickly. "We'd better clarify a few things in this matter."

"All right, all right, but sit down and wait a few minutes while I clean up. I've got to get all this stage makeup off," Mr. Rushton said.

"Well, don't take too long in there. We've got to do something about this—fast," the man replied.

There was the sound of a door closing inside the suite.

Mandie moved back on tiptoe and motioned for her friends to follow. When they were far enough away from the suite to talk, she whispered to them, "I just can't believe it! That good-looking Mr. Rushton is a thief!" she exclaimed softly.

"Imagine a famous man doing a thing like that," Jonathan added.

"We'd better get back to the table, Mandie. Mr. Swaggingham may come looking for us," Celia cautioned her friend.

"No," Mandie quickly replied. "Not right now, Celia. I've got to think what we should do. No one will believe us if we go and repeat what we heard."

"Why not?" Jonathan asked. "There are three of us who heard it all."

"Well, I guess I'm afraid of Mr. Rushton now. He might do something to us," Mandie said in a nervous voice.

"Like what? If we go tell Mr. Swaggingham what we heard, he'll see that the men are arrested," Jonathan argued.

"I don't know," Mandie said, impatiently waving her

hand in the air. She paced up and down the hallway a short distance as she pondered what she had heard. Jonathan and Celia silently stood waiting.

To think that a man she had admired had turned out to be a thief! She was always getting into trouble with strangers. Maybe some day she'd learn how to evaluate a person. But then her grandmother had also been enthused over Mr. Rushton's performance. And he seemed to enjoy a lot of popularity in Rome. Why had he done such a thing? It would completely destroy his career, becoming involved with a criminal like that.

Suddenly, something dawned on Mandie. She came to a halt and hurried toward her friends. "You know what? I think Mr. Rushton has that ruby!" she whispered excitedly. "He took it out of my old bag! That's why he offered to have his maid wash it for me!"

Jonathan nodded slowly. "And now he's deceiving his friend," he said.

"Yes, he told the man he didn't know anything about it," Celia agreed.

"We've got to figure out what we should do," Mandie said, cuddling Snowball. "If we could somehow let that other man know that Mr. Rushton has the ruby, they could fight it out between them."

"They might just kill each other over such a thing," Jonathan decided.

"But, Mandie, we don't have to get them fighting over the stone," Celia objected.

"Yes, we do. We have to let that other man know Mr. Rushton has the ruby because if we tell the police, Mr. Rushton will go scot-free. He'll lie and put it all off on the other man," Mandie explained.

"Well, if you are planning to go into his suite, count

me out," Celia told her. "I'll wait here in the hall."

"Jonathan, help me think," Mandie said, turning to him.

"You're right about Mr. Rushton, Mandie, but I don't know exactly what we can do," Jonathan said.

"We've got to think of something," Mandie said, beginning to pace the hallway again. "Help me, Jonathan. Something has to be done, and right away."

Chapter 12 / Unexpected Help

Several people passed along the hallway and looked at the young people. But as Mandie paced the floor, deep in thought, she hardly noticed their curious stares.

Snowball squirmed as he tried to get down.

Mandie scolded him crossly. Then suddenly, she got an idea. Hurrying to her friends, she explained what she was going to do. "Let's listen at the door again to be sure Mr. Rushton is back in the room with the other man," Mandie told them, hurrying toward the suite.

"This could be dangerous, Mandie," Jonathan cautioned.

"Not if we all stick together," Mandie replied. "Besides, there are lots of other people around. Haven't you noticed?" She removed Snowball's red leash from his harness, rolled it up, and put it in her pocket.

As they neared the door, they tiptoed and looked around to be sure no one else in the corridor saw them eavesdropping. Mandie stood close to the door.

The two men were talking again.

"I found the old lady's keys and unlocked the girls' trunks, looking for the stone, and it was nowhere to be found," the foreigner was saying. "At least I snatched the old lady's ruby necklace for you. That's got to be worth something."

Mandie and Celia gasped and looked at each other. Mandie's face turned red with anger. She motioned to her friends, and the three walked a short distance away from the door.

"Now, I'm going to race up there and shove Snowball through the door, and run back and start calling him," Mandie explained. "Then I'll just nonchalantly push open Mr. Rushton's door to look for him. Understand?"

Jonathan and Celia nodded.

Mandie hurried to carry out her plan. She ran back to Mr. Rushton's partly opened door and pushed Snowball through the crack into the suite. She rushed back to her friends, and started calling the kitten, "Snowball, Snowball, where are you?" she called loudly. She hurried toward the door. "Snowball, did you go in there? Where are you?" She pushed the door open and looked into the room.

George Rushton and the other man were sitting in the parlor, talking. They jumped up. Snowball wandered on into the back of the room.

Mandie pretended surprise at seeing Mr. Rushton. "Oh, I'm sorry," she apologized. "I think my kitten ran in here."

George Rushton caught sight of Snowball and reached for him. "Yes, yes, here he is."

But the kitten evaded his grasp.

Jonathan and Celia stood in the doorway. The door was now wide open.

"I'll get him," Mandie said. As she reached for Snowball, she noticed the jewelry case sitting on the table behind the chair where Mr. Rushton had been sitting. Instead of picking up her cat, she picked up the case and opened it. Inside was the ruby the magician had used in his second performance. "Oh, this is beautiful!" she cried.

George Rushton quickly grabbed the case from her. "Sorry, Miss, I don't allow anyone to touch that," he said.

"It looks so real," Mandie exclaimed, picking up Snowball. "In fact, I think I've seen it before."

The magician closed the case and held it tightly in both his hands. "Yes, you have seen it before. It's the stone I use in my magic show," he told her. "Now if you don't mind, my friend and I were involved in a business deal."

"A business deal? Oh, are you going into another business?" Mandie asked innocently. She looked at the other man. "Business like—"

Jonathan quickly cut her off. "Mandie, we've got to go now. Come on!" He spoke sharply.

Celia peeked out from behind Jonathan. "Yes, Mr. Rushton is busy," she added.

The magician turned and placed the jewelry case on the table as he sat down. "It was nice seeing you again, Miss Shaw, but right now I have business to take care of."

Mandie moved close to Celia in the doorway and handed Snowball to her. Her friend looked at her questioningly. Then Mandie quickly stepped back into the room and snatched up the case. "This is the ruby you two stole from the catacombs," she shouted to the foreigner. "And Mr. Rushton stole it out of my bag."

She ran from the room after her friends who had quickly exited. With shaking hands, she hastily opened the case, grabbed the ruby, and dropped the case to the floor. Racing down the hall, she glanced back. The two men were close behind her. Her heart pounded.

Just then she nearly collided with someone. It was Uncle Ned, her dear old Cherokee friend! She dropped the ruby into the sling of arrows the Indian carried on his shoulder. Uncle Ned grasped her to keep from falling and rushed along with her.

Mandie looked back and spotted the strange woman from the ship. The woman put out a sharp-toed shoe and tripped the foreigner, who fell flat on his face.

The woman smiled at Mandie and said, "You see? I am your friend." And she quickly disappeared down the corridor.

"Papoose!" the old Indian exclaimed. "What happen here?"

"Oh, Uncle Ned!" Mandie cried. "I'm so glad you're here."

George Rushton caught up with Mandie. He stopped short when he saw Uncle Ned. "An Indian? What are you doing here?"

Suddenly, out of nowhere, Mr. Swaggingham appeared. He quickly threw George Rushton to the floor beside the other man who seemed unable to get up.

Mr. Rushton looked up at Mandie from the floor. Now that she had protection, Mandie bent to speak to him, "You know, you broke one of the Ten Commandments: 'Thou shalt not steal.' "

The man's face grew pale. He didn't reply.

Mr. Swaggingham also tied up the foreigner and then turned to the young people. "Your grandmother is going to be awfully upset with all this," he told Mandie. "I don't know exactly what's going on except that these two men were chasing all of you and seemed bent on inflicting some kind of harm."

After quickly explaining to Uncle Ned and the detective what had happened, Mandie introduced the two men.

Mr. Swaggingham shook hands with Uncle Ned. "I've always wanted to see a real live Indian," he said, smiling.

The old Indian smiled back.

"Well, I'm also one-fourth Cherokee, you know," Mandie said proudly. Looking down the corridor she saw several uniformed men hurrying toward them. "Here come the police!"

When the policemen got within hearing, everyone started talking at once.

Mandie tried to talk to Uncle Ned amid the hustle and bustle, but the policemen were intent on questioning her and her friends.

A young policeman picked up the jewelry case and showed it to Mandie. "Do you know if this belongs to Mr. Rushton?" he asked.

"Yes, it does," Mandie replied. Then, reaching down into Uncle Ned's sling, she pulled out the ruby and handed it to the man. "This was inside the box when I grabbed it and ran out of his room."

The man looked at the ruby and let out a low whistle. He spoke in rapid Italian to his fellow policemen, and they gathered around to look.

Mandie could guess what they were saying, but to be sure, she said, "Yes, that's the ruby stolen from the catacombs."

"*Sí, sí, Signorina,*" the policeman said with a big grin. "Yes, yes."

Some of the policemen had gone into Rushton's suite. They came out with a bag full of jewelry, which they told her had been reported missing from various places in Italy.

"You have caught the most clever thief we have ever known," the young policeman told Mandie as he displayed the contents of the bag.

One piece of jewelry caught her eye. She reached for it." This is my grandmother's ruby necklace!" she exclaimed.

The policeman looked sharply at her. "Your grandmother's?" he asked. "How can we be sure?"

"I don't know how to identify it except that I do know it's my grandmother's and hers is missing," Mandie insisted as she fingered the beautiful necklace.

Uncle Ned and Jonathan and Celia all spoke at once, confirming that it belonged to Mrs. Taft.

The policeman hesitated, looking from one to the other. "But we must have some means of identification," the man insisted. He reached to take it back from Mandie.

At that moment, Mrs. Taft and Senator Morton came into the hallway from the front door. They stopped in alarm as they viewed the two men tied up on the floor and all the policemen standing around.

Mrs. Taft rushed to Mandie and her friends. "What is going on? What has happened?" she demanded.

Mandie, Jonathan, and Celia tried to piece the story together for her. The policeman patiently stood by, waiting for Mandie to give back the ruby necklace. Then Mandie realized she was still holding it.

"Grandmother, here's your ruby necklace," Mandie told her. "The police found it and a lot of other jewelry in George Rushton's room."

Mrs. Taft gasped and took the necklace from Mandie. "My, oh my, I never would have thought such a thing of the man!" she said. "Of course, I'm very glad to have it back."

The policeman cleared his throat and reached for the necklace. "I'm sorry, madam," he said, "but we have to have some proof that the necklace actually belongs to you, please."

"Proof?" Mrs. Taft puzzled as the man took the necklace. "Why, that necklace has been in our family for several generations. In fact, the clasp is so old, it's hard to fasten. Part of the little circle on it is missing."

The policeman examined the clasp. He smiled and handed it back to Mrs. Taft. "I am sorry, madam, but I had to make sure," he said. "Your description is sufficient proof. I am glad to return it to you."

She thanked him and carefully put the necklace into her bag as the policemen led the magician and his accomplice away. Then she saw Uncle Ned and gasped in astonishment. "Why, Uncle Ned! Were you in on all this too?" she asked.

The old Indian shook his head. "Man at desk tell me Papoose go to number 100. When I look, I find man chasing Papoose."

Mrs. Taft turned to her granddaughter in shock. "That man chased you, Amanda?"

"Yes, Grandmother. After I snatched his jewelry case, he tried to catch me," Mandie explained.

Mrs. Taft turned pale.

Mr. Swaggingham spoke up. "Don't worry, Mrs. Taft. The young people didn't know it, but when they left me in the dining room to go to the restrooms, I followed them. I didn't trust them not to go meddling in something after all I had heard them talk about. I was right here behind that post all the time. And I was armed." He patted a lump in his coat pocket.

"Thank goodness!" Mrs. Taft said.

The young people looked at him in disbelief.

"But why didn't we see you?" Mandie asked the detective.

"Because I am trained not to be seen," the man explained. "When you first went to eavesdrop at that man's door, I knew you were up to something, so I just stood there ready to protect you."

"I think we'd better find a place to sit," Mrs. Taft said. "With all this excitement I suddenly feel faint."

Senator Morton quickly took Mrs. Taft's arm and led the way into the dining room. Uncle Ned stayed close by Mandie.

Mandie squeezed the old man's wrinkled hand. "Oh, Uncle Ned, you just don't know how glad I was to see you," she said.

"Papoose must not do dangerous things," Uncle Ned scolded. "What happen if I not be there . . . if detective man not be there?"

"I know, Uncle Ned. I'm sorry," Mandie said. Then she brightened. "Rome has been so exciting, but we're leaving tomorrow for Switzerland."

"I know," he said with a twinkle in his eyes.

"We're going to stay in a real house over there," Mandie explained. "A chalet, they call it. We won't be in a hotel like this."

"I know, Papoose." The Indian nodded.

Mandie looked up at her old friend and said, "You always know everything. Tell us who that strange woman is who shows up almost everywhere we go. She always seems to be following us."

Uncle Ned shook his head. "I not know," he admitted.

Mandie sighed in frustration. "That woman tripped the foreign-looking man awhile ago when he was chasing me, and then she looked at me and said she was our friend," Mandie puzzled. "It's all so strange. Have you ever seen her, Uncle Ned?"

The old Indian shrugged. "Not know who you talk about."

The waiter brought tea for everyone, and the conversation centered around the theft and the man they had all thought to be above reproach.

"It's such a disappointment to learn of a person's dishonesty," Mrs. Taft said sadly.

One of the policemen joined them at the table and explained the situation. "Mr. Rushton's career was failing. He was nearly bankrupt and heavily in debt. He began dealings with this thief about a year ago from what we've been able to determine," the policeman told them. "The bag of jewelry we found in his room contained some of the most valuable pieces ever to be stolen, and they are from several different countries. We can't imagine how he was going to get rid of them unless he knew someone who could recut them. But then maybe he didn't and that's why he still had all the jewels."

They all talked for a while about the theft, and the policeman apologized for any inconvenience caused them while they were guests of Rome. Finally, he told them he would have to leave and make his report. He stood, saluted them at the table, and bowed slightly. As he left the room, he called out, "*Arrivederci!*"

Instinctively knowing that he was saying goodbye, the whole group called out, "Goodbye, and thanks."

When they had all finished their tea, Mr. Swaggingham asked, "Mrs. Taft, do you wish me to stay tonight now that the mystery has been solved?"

"What do you think, Senator?" Mrs. Taft asked her friend.

"Yes, I think it would be a good idea," Senator Morton advised. "There could be another accomplice that the police don't know about."

They all rose from the table to go upstairs.

"We'd feel safer with Mr. Swaggingham in the parlor, Grandmother," Mandie said.

"That's right," Celia added.

Mandie turned to her Cherokee friend. "Unless Uncle Ned could sleep on the sofa in our parlor tonight."

The old Indian shook his head. "Other business tonight, Papoose," he said.

"Oh, shucks, Uncle Ned. I was hoping you'd be around for a while," Mandie said, looking up at the old man.

"Back tomorrow," the Indian promised.

"But we're leaving early in the morning, aren't we, Grandmother?" Mandie asked.

"Yes, dear, right after breakfast," Mrs. Taft replied.

"Back before breakfast," he promised her. "Ned be ready to go Swissyland with Papoose."

Mandie's blue eyes grew big. "You are going to Switzerland with us?" she exclaimed. "Oh, Uncle Ned, I'm so happy."

Jonathan spoke up, "Yes, we're glad you're coming along with us, sir."

"House in Swissyland have mystery," Uncle Ned said with a laugh. "Ned go see Papoose not get into trouble."

Mandie stopped in surprise. "The house in Switzerland has a mystery about it?" she asked. "Oh, that's just great!"

"We see, Papoose," the old Indian said. "Sun come up, Ned come."

That night as Mandie and Celia lay in bed, they were

so excited about the events of that day and about the new mystery in Switzerland that they could hardly get to sleep.

Finally, Mandie closed her eyes. *Oh, I can't wait to get to Switzerland!* she thought. *What kind of a mystery could there be about the house?*

With Special Acknowledgment

To Signor Nuzzo Vittorio, Office of the Ambassador of Italy, Washington, D.C., for furnishing research material on his country and information on the history of Rome. Grazie!